'Regrets

With a sud front
of her, tipp ers.

'Of course not! How could I egret
becoming your wife?'

'I don't know, Caterina.' Nicolò's quiet answer sent a spasm of apprehension down her spine as she became unbearably aware of the closeness of his very male body. 'But I warn you against it, because I shall never let you go. What I have, I hold.'

Dear Reader

In February, we celebrate one of the most romantic times of the year—St Valentine's Day, when messages of true love are exchanged. At Mills & Boon we feel that our novels carry the Valentine spirit on throughout the year and we hope that readers agree. Dipping into the pages of our books will give you a taste of true romance every month... so chase away those winter blues and look forward to spring with Mills & Boon!

Till next month,

The Editor

Angela Wells was educated in an Essex convent, and later left the bustling world of media marketing and advertising to marry and start a family in a suburb of London. Writing started out as a hobby, and she uses backgrounds she knows well from her many travels, especially in the Mediterranean area. Her ambition, she says, in addition to writing many more romances, is to spend more time in Australia—especially Sydney and the islands of the Great Barrier Reef.

Recent titles by the same author:

VIKING MAGIC

GOLDEN MISTRESS

BY

ANGELA WELLS

MILLS & BOON

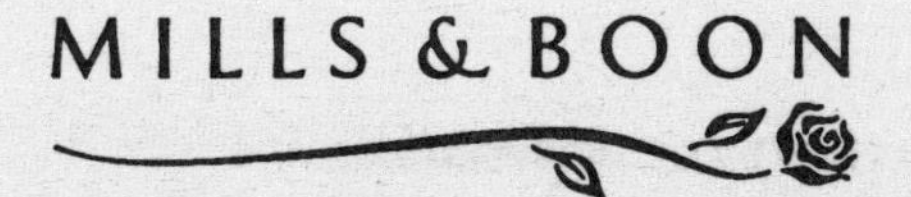

MILLS & BOON LIMITED
ETON HOUSE, 18-24 PARADISE ROAD
RICHMOND, SURREY TW9 1SR

First published in Great Britain 1993
by Mills & Boon Limited

This edition 1994

ISBN 0 263 78399 5

Set in Times Roman 10 on 12 pt.
01-9402-54606 C

Made and printed in Great Britain

CHAPTER ONE

NICOLÒ didn't love her. Her eyes a blur of tears, Catia stared out of the window of the Boeing 737 somewhere high over Europe as it sped towards Venice and the start of her honeymoon. Serene skies and a view unmarked by clouds were in direct contrast to the turbulence which raged in her heart. Nervously the fingers of her right hand played with the twisted band of diamonds and rubies on the third finger of her other hand. At ten o'clock that morning she'd been the happiest girl alive—or so she'd imagined, as the handsome man who had courted her with such speed and seeming devotion had placed his ring on her finger.

Conscious of his warm, vibrant presence beside her, her body tensed as she fastened her gaze resolutely on the passing landscape beneath her. There was no way she dared look at him or the bitter tears of anger and pain would betray her. How had she managed to contain her grief for so long? she wondered. Probably because her grandfather's guileless farewell had forced her into a catatonic state, she surmised, so that she'd moved like a zombie through the airport formalities, shown little reaction at the announcement that their flight had been delayed by air-traffic control problems over Europe, and, claiming a tiredness which was only half faked, had closed her eyes and pretended to rest in the club class lounge at Heathrow.

She had had doubts at first about her growing attraction towards Nicolò. Of course she had. The quiet life she had led with Nonno and her great-aunt Becky in the small Suffolk village where they lived had hardly prepared her for a glitzy social existence, with the opportunity of meeting a selection of young men. The few she had met during her teenage years and afterwards, during the first year of her career as a physiotherapist at a large London hospital, hadn't managed to inspire any deep feelings within her, but at twenty-two, just starting her career, she'd been perfectly contented with her life.

Perhaps, she accorded sadly, if she'd experienced and recovered from an attack of calf-love in her formative years she would have been better able to deal with Nicolò Cacciatore! But she'd resolved to live the kind of life that wouldn't offend the strict standards of the elderly couple who had cherished her since babyhood. Not that she'd ever ached for the sexual freedom so many of her contemporaries enjoyed—or seemed to enjoy on the surface. She'd seen enough emotional trauma to have reservations about whether the brief pleasures were worth so much pain when they vanished!

Yet her reluctance to experiment had left her vulnerable to the first renegade who had mounted an attack on her unprepared heart. Nicolò Cacciatore had captured her—heart and soul—by storm two months earlier.

Her fingernails dug into her palms as she remembered that first meeting, Nonno coming to greet her at the door of the country house to which he'd brought her after the tragic death of her parents in Italy when she'd been two years of age. He had been smiling and her heart had lifted at the sight, because for several months previously he had appeared dispirited and depressed. In fact it had been worry about his state of health which had prompted her to take her annual holiday so early in the year. She swallowed deeply in an attempt to control her emotions as she recalled the events of that day.

She'd barely had time to greet her grandfather and Aunt Becky when the door to the pleasant, sunny sitting-room had opened and a stranger had appeared on the scene. And what a stranger! Even now she could remember how she must have gaped at the presence of such unparalleled masculine beauty. Six feet two of powerful bone and muscle clothed in a fawn and oatmeal mixture lightweight woollen tweed suit, a silk patterned tie neatly knotted at the neck of his toning check shirt, he looked, every beautifully honed piece of flesh and sinew of him, the successful businessman she'd later discovered him to be.

'Nicolò Cacciatore.' Nonno had smiled delightedly as he'd made the introductions. 'My granddaughter, Caterina!'

Nicolò had stepped forward, extending his hand in greeting, dipping his dark head in acknowledgement of her presence before pinioning her flushed face with the sombre darkness of his eyes. Almost unwillingly her attention had been drawn to the thickness of his long, dark eyelashes with their surprisingly golden tips as their hands had clasped.

In her profession she dealt with all ages and conditions of mankind and she didn't need her disturbing visitor to take off his clothing to be aware that he was a near perfect specimen of *Homo sapiens* in his early thirties. Perfect, that was, in the sense of muscular and orthopaedic development.

'It gives me great pleasure to meet you at last, *signorina*.' The long, spatulate fingers had hardened around her palm, his expression alert, his mouth pleasantly curved in welcome, yet behind the dark lustre of his eyes something lingered to encourage the fluctuation of her pulse.

'I don't think my grandfather has ever mentioned you to me, *signore*,' she had returned coolly, shooting a reproachful glance at Antonio Laurence's complacent face.

'Probably because this is the first time we have met in the flesh, so to speak,' Nicolò had said smoothly. 'But our families have long since been acquainted, and, be assured, the reputation of your charm and beauty has preceded our meeting.' His dark eyes had glittered as he'd taken up her challenge.

Too practised, too slick! Now, when it was too late, she knew she had been a fool to fall for such a line. But then . . .

Then she'd been transfixed by his pure magnetism, allowing her senses their freedom as her grandfather had ushered them back into the sitting-room, his expression bland and relaxed, belying his eighty-seven years, and the tragedy which had robbed him of his only son in a power-boat explosion on the Italian lakes twenty years previously.

'Nicolò's the son of an old friend of mine,' he'd informed her blithely as Aunt Becky had entered the room, bearing a tray on which a bottle of champagne dominated four crystal champagne flutes. 'He's over here on business at the moment and decided to look me up.' Taking the bottle, Antonio Laurence had unwound the metal constraints, thumbing the cork towards the ceiling, where it had marked the plaster as the wine foamed into the glasses.

'My company in Milan is one of the foremost names in automobile engineering,' Nicolò had informed her easily as he'd accepted the glass proffered by her grandfather. 'The purpose of my visit to this country was to liaise with your top mechanical engineers and at the same time discover what the British motorist really wants in a new car.'

'As opposed to what you think he or she should want?' An imp of mischief had tempted her to challenge his vanity as a self-designated expert. She'd been rewarded by a rueful quirk of his lips.

'It's a mistake to underestimate the intelligence of one's customer.'

'Or one's prey?'

The tart remark had burst from her lips without conscious thought, an instinctive response to her inner awareness that the name of Cacciatore, when translated into its English equivalent, mirrored his personality. Hunter by name—hunter by nature. Even then something deep within her had recognised that he was dangerous. How dangerous, she had only just discovered.

'The ultimate disaster,' he had agreed, nodding his sable head in agreement, the thick dark hair sculpted by the hand of an artist against the contours of a perfectly balanced skull, his dark gaze continuing to bathe her in its regard as he'd lifted the glass to his lips, pre-empting any toast her grandfather might have been about to make. 'To our friendship, Caterina.'

Friendship? Privately she doubted if Nicolò Cacciatore had ever had a woman friend since celebrating his fourteenth birthday! But then had not been the time to dispute it. Not with Nonno and Aunt Becky smiling and raising their glasses. So she had obediently followed suit, clinking her glass with his, before sipping deeply at the effervescent liquid, feeling the bubbles sting her palate.

It was impossible to identify the precise moment she'd fallen in love with Nicolò. She supposed there'd been clues in the fluctuations of her emotions almost from the first day he had thrust himself into her life, but, like the crocuses which bloomed each spring beneath the apple trees in her grandfather's garden at Suddingham, they had stayed unperceived by her, maturing in the deep, dark recesses where they'd been planted, until one day they'd flowered in all their golden glory, refusing to be denied.

That moment she recalled perfectly. Nicolò had expressed a wish to purchase a colt from the local bloodstock agent, their friend and neighbour Richard Carville, with the aim of putting it into training and running it in Europe in the colours of his company, and it had been at the beginning of the second week of her holiday that he'd finally made his choice. The weather had been glorious, the promise of spring tangible in the sudden flourish of unfurled leaves and the light blossom of the cherry trees.

She'd returned to Richard's stables after a pulse-raising canter on Treasure, Richard's own chestnut mare, glowing with happiness and satisfaction after her exertions, her whole body tingling with the pure joy of being alive and healthy.

Dismounted, she'd just handed over the chestnut to Richard's resident groom when Nicolò's voice had hailed her. Turning to face him, she'd realised the truth with a similar shock to her system as that which must have been experienced by Saul on the road to Damascus.

It had been inevitable that they should spend a great deal of their time together during her stay in Suddingham since he was Nonno's honoured guest. She'd enjoyed his company as gradually, with a mixture of Latin charm and brooding masculinity, he had overcome the natural caution which was a facet of her temperament to insinuate himself into her mind and heart.

He'd read her capitulation in the instant her gaze had alighted on him, and she'd been lost. Shuddering beneath the caressing sweep of his hands as he'd pulled her into his embrace, she'd been powerless to escape the possessive intensity of his lips. Overtaken by sensation as his sweetly searching tongue found sanctuary in the warm darkness of her mouth, she'd experienced the awakening of a savage physical hunger.

She hadn't known which was worse—the warm, aroused masculine scent of his skin, the erotic taste of him or the feel of his fingers imprinting themselves against the soft leather jacket which covered her shoulders—but she'd responded by digging her own fingers into the sensitive area of his back, her senses thrilling as he'd responded by raising his hands to her hair, threading them through the long wavy strands of blonde silk, imprisoning her head so that she'd had to press even closer against him, forcing her to lift her face as the heat of his body transmitted itself to her. The first law of thermodynamics, she'd thought deliriously, recalling the physics lessons of her college days—or was it the second? Heat always passed from a warmer body to a colder one...

It had been several minutes later, after he'd released her from his powerful embrace, that the full implications of the flowering of her love for Nicolò Cacciatore had registered with her.

'How soon will you marry me?' he had asked her softly, yet with the underlying arrogance of the conqueror. In retrospect she should have heeded the warning lurking in the triumphant sparkle of his night-dark eyes. But she hadn't. Assailed by a sudden faintness, she had grasped at his upper arms, her feelings torn between her undoubted desire for Nicolò and her loyalty towards her grandfather, to whom she owed so much and whose need for her was different from but surely greater than Nicolò's?

'Nonno...' she had whispered from dry lips. 'He would never approve.' Torn between love and duty, she'd wondered how she'd ever be able to make Nicolò understand her grandfather's inexplicable attitude towards the country and culture of his birth, when she didn't fully understand it herself.

She'd half expected Nicolò to be irritated, angry even, to point out that she was old enough to make her own decisions, live her own life, but his reaction had surprised her, as she'd struggled to find the words she needed.

'No problem.' He had laced long, sensuous fingers through her wind-tousled hair and brushed her warm cheek with his gentle mouth. 'I'll ask your grandfather for his blessing, and, if he refuses, then I'll return to Italy without you...if you tell me that is what you want.'

At the end of the week he'd done precisely that—returned to Italy without her. But his departure hadn't been because Antonio Laurence had rejected him as her suitor, but because he'd given them both his blessing and Nicolò had returned to Milan to put his business affairs in order before returning to England for their June wedding.

She clenched her teeth, swallowing the sudden surge of bitterness which assailed her tongue. She'd thought at the time that she'd known all the important things about her husband-to-be. He'd told her his mother was the second and much younger wife of his elderly father, and that the first marriage, which had ended in widowerhood for his father, had been unproductive. Because his father was fifty when he was born, Nicolò's arrival had been greeted with unalloyed joy and thanksgiving, and since he'd remained an only child he'd received lavish affection and financial support from his parents as he'd studied for his qualifications.

Her delicate query as to why he'd waited until his early thirties before marrying had been met with the blithe assurance that he'd been waiting for that sublime moment when he would look across a room and know without doubt that he'd seen his future wife. Because it had been what she'd wanted to believe she'd accepted the explanation at face value. Not that she'd suspected him of inexperience where women were concerned. Nicolò Cacciatore was no amateur in the delicate art of love—*that* she'd already known—although his total expertise she had yet to discover.

Then, she had believed she'd understood and shared his taste in art and music, in literature and food, known what made him laugh and what provoked him to righteous indignation. She had sensed that behind his air of forcefulness there lurked a compassionate heart—and she'd been wrong. If only she'd realised then what she now knew—that Nicolò's apparent deference to her grandfather's wishes had been based on the cynical awareness that the older man would raise no objection to their union because of circumstances beyond his control.

It had been her grandfather who had insisted that they have a civil wedding in England before they left for Italy and the full panoply of a religious service. She'd been glad to comply so that her friends from the hospital and her neighbours could witness her happiness. Later, Nicolò had promised her they would make their vows in front of his friends and family in Venice...and of course Nonno and Aunt Becky would fly over for the occasion.

Right up until the moment she'd stood beside him in the local register office she'd still hardly been able to credit that her grandfather had given his blessing, not reluctantly, but with obvious approval. Since his only son's death and his decision to bring his granddaughter to England to be raised in the joint custody of himself and his daughter-in-law's aunt, Antonio Laurence had shown a bitterness towards the country of his birth and his fellow citizens that she'd privately considered bordered on the neurotic, even changing his family name of Lorenzo to the anglicised version by which he was now known, and becoming angry when she'd told him of her decision to take Italian as a second language for her A levels.

In answer to her hesitant enquiry at the time as to his change of heart about his fellow countrymen, he'd reassured her with a benign smile.

'As I grow older my desire to see the country of my birth once more grows stronger and I begin to realise that my previous judgements and grief were perhaps a little too biased. Certainly not valid enough to stand in the way of the happiness of my only granddaughter!' he'd confided. 'Nicolò Cacciatore is a wealthy man. He will make you a good husband.'

Wealthy! As if that were a base for happiness! But at the time she'd been so happy that she'd never thought to query her grandfather's oddly voiced approval. Confident that Nicolò loved her as much as she loved him—why else did a man propose marriage?—she'd gone to her wedding in a blaze of euphoria, only to taste the ashes of disillusionment a few hours later.

Even now she could hardly bear to relive the scene she'd stumbled on as the small reception held at home had drawn to an end. Aware that she and Nicolò would be leaving to catch their plane for Venice within the hour, she'd come lightly downstairs, after having repaired her make-up and re-coiled her long hair into a sophisticated sweep, when she'd heard Nicolò's voice coming from her grandfather's study.

Without a second thought she'd gone to join him, the deep-pile carpet absorbing the sound of her high heels. On the point of fully opening the heavy door which stood a few inches ajar, some sixth sense had brought her to a halt. She loved her grandfather dearly and accepted that, not unnaturally at his advanced age, he was one of the old school of macho Italians who, while appreciating their womenfolk, also insisted in enjoying a male camaraderie from which the former were excluded. If he and Nicolò were talking 'men's talk' her sudden appearance might embarrass him. With a wry smile she'd been about to turn away when her grandfather had spoken, his voice low and intense.

'You realise I would never have considered an arranged marriage if I hadn't been certain it was in Catia's best interests.'

And then the deep timbre of Nicolò's reply. 'Relax, Antonio, you have done nothing to be ashamed of. Caterina will have wealth and position as my wife, everything you would want her to enjoy.'

'And you swear you will never tell her that this marriage came about because of an outstanding debt of honour between our families?' Her grandfather's voice had shaken, betraying both guilt and regret to her incredulous ears.

'It would hardly be in my best interests, would it?' There had been a lilt of amusement in Nicolò's answer that had struck at her heart. She had turned, unable to bear hearing more, running upstairs to the sanctuary of her bedroom, the evil words echoing in her mind. 'Arranged marriage...' 'Outstanding debt of honour...'

It was unbelievable! Nicolò had married her because he loved her, hadn't he? But the words she had overheard were engraved in her memory and, twist them though she tried, there was no other meaning to them. Nicolò had come to England with the sole intent of calling in a favour, and that favour had been her hand in marriage. Her dearly loved and devoted grandfather had sold her in order to preserve his own idea of honour. But why would Nicolò have wanted her? What could she offer him that he hadn't been able to find among his fellow countrywomen?

Sightlessly she had stared at her reflection, not seeing the pallidity of her cheeks or the dullness of her normally sparkling blue eyes. It was not too late to escape the bondage into which she'd gone so carelessly. True, she was legally married, but her union wasn't recognised by the church. She could run away, disappear, refuse to live with Nicolò Cacciatore. The marriage could be annulled on the grounds of non-consummation.

A knock at the door had disturbed her train of reasoning as Aunt Becky had entered the room.

'Are you nearly ready, love?' Twelve years younger than Antonio, Becky had given her a sweet smile. 'The chauffeur's outside, ready to take you to the airport.'

However grave her grandfather's behaviour, how could she disrupt the lives of these two people who had loved and guided her for the past twenty years? Aunt Becky almost certainly had been no party to the deception, yet she too would suffer if her niece created a scandal. And what of Antonio Laurence himself? How much had he been indebted to the Cacciatore family? Had he owed them money he'd been unable to repay?

Nonno was eighty-seven and comparatively frail. She'd shuddered, recalling the recent deterioration in his health. Perhaps his flight from Italy all those years ago had been caused by more than the death of his son. Now the past had caught up with him, because he would never have traded her future unless the alternative had been too ugly to contemplate.

'Catia, my dear, are you all right?' Becky had taken one of her hands and chafed the cold skin. 'Is something wrong?'

'Of course not, Aunt Becky!' She'd made the effort to stretch her lips into a smile and rise to her feet. There could be no going back. No way she could tell either Nonno or her husband what she had overheard, for fear that the consequences would spread disaster among all those she loved.

'Ladies and gentlemen, we shall be landing at Marco Polo Airport, Venice, in a few minutes' time. We apologise for the long delay before take-off...'

The disembodied voice above her head continued, but Catia no longer heard it, as the full panoply of the floating city spread out beneath the plane. Choked by the powerful mix of emotions which seethed inside her, among which anger was predominant, she was scarcely aware of Nicolò's hands tightening her seatbelt as the Boeing made its descent. How long she'd dreamed of this moment, imagining the joy and excitement she would feel as she trod on Italian soil for the first time in the presence of the man she loved.

So much for dreams! She might be a pawn in an unknown game, but she was no simpleton to be manoeuvred by rules she didn't understand. For the first time since she had unwittingly eavesdropped, anger replaced the despair in her heart. Whatever Nicolò's motive had been in coming all the way from Italy intent on marrying a woman he'd never met, she would discover it.

It was something to which she would give her priority attention she determined grimly, because until she found out what hold Nicolò had over her grandfather she would be unable to devise a plan to escape from the impossible position into which she'd walked blindfold. Supposing she hadn't fallen in love with Nicolò? What then? she wondered. Would Nonno have taken her into his confidence and begged her compliance?

The question was hypothetical. Nicolò was a vitally attractive man and that, allied to the character and personality he had assumed to woo her, had made the outcome a foregone conclusion. For the first time in her life she regretted not having played the field where men were concerned. That way she would have been less gullible, more sceptical about the sudden appearance in her life of a handsome stranger!

Her resolution hardened. Nicolò might think he had won the game, and obviously she would have to tread warily, but her pride demanded that she attack his smugness in victory. Suppose he should discover that instead of catching some soft, compliant victim in his trap he had ensnared a vixen? Perhaps he might regret his action and be prepared to let her go. It was a faint hope, but one she must cling on to, because no way did she intend to spend the rest of her life in a loveless marriage!

Nicolò Cacciatore was going to find out that there was more to his previously naïve, docile new bride than he had ever imagined. Much more!

CHAPTER TWO

In a surprisingly short space of time they were through Customs and outside the small air terminal, where Nicolò ignored the waiting *vaporetto* which moved leisurely in the gentle lapping waters of the canal and to which the other airline passengers were making their way, leading her instead to another jetty against which a private launch was moored.

'*Signore*! At last!' A swarthy man of indeterminate age clasped Nicolò's hand. 'My congratulations to you and the *signora* . . .' The handclasp was moved to embrace Catia.

'Have we kept you waiting long, Giovanni?' Nicolò handed over their luggage, before assisting Catia into the craft.

The other man grimaced. 'I checked with the airport before leaving the *palazzo*. But for a while I was concerned you would not arrive in time to welcome your guests.'

'*Palazzo*? Guests?' Dismay added to her turbulent emotions. How could she cope with entertaining when she already had so much on her mind? She sank down on the soft cushions of the covered cabin as the launch purred smoothly away from its mooring, espying a recalcitrant speck of confetti clinging to one nylon-covered leg as she did so, and brushing it off. She'd removed every single fragment from the simple ecru-coloured silk suit she'd chosen for her earlier register office wedding, but had obviously underestimated the attractive quality of nylon!

'Mmm.' Nicolò lounged down beside her. 'We'll be sharing our own deluxe apartment in one of the twelfth-century *palazzi* fronting the Grand Canal.'

'You mean self-catering?' Drawing the remaining shreds of her self-esteem around her as she spoke the first words in the part she had allotted herself to play, she managed to endow the suggestion with a hint of offended disdain. 'Couldn't you afford a proper hotel?' she demanded peevishly. 'I hadn't anticipated spending my honeymoon doing chores.'

'Neither shall you have to,' Nicolò assured her, raising his eyebrows at her querulous expression. 'The apartment comes fully inclusive of its own staff, prepared to wait on us hand and foot, twenty-four hours a day.'

'Thank heavens for that! I thought for a moment that I'd made a dreadful mistake and tied myself up to a miser. Was it very expensive to organise?'

'Actually, no.' A slight frown marred his broad forehead as he regarded her avid face. 'In a manner of speaking I own the *palazzo*—at least my company does. We rescued it from decay and ignominy about ten years ago, with the backing of the bank, and restored it to something of its previous glory on the outside. Inside——' he made an expressive gesture with his hands, '—well, we had to make some concessions to modernity, but the ground floor has been turned into a ballroom which reflects much of the former opulence of the *palazzo* and is hired out for functions. The first floor contains apartments for visitors and clients and above that we have offices.'

'I see,' Catia said faintly, not quite sure what she did see. Nicolò was full of surprises! Not only had he persuaded her beloved grandfather into making a human sacrifice of her, but he now appeared much more wealthy than she had originally supposed, despite her pretence to the contrary. The next thing he would be telling her was that he was some kind of Venetian princeling! Although surely he had told her his family had originally come from much further south?

'Good.' His murmur met her ear. 'I'm glad I haven't disappointed your expectations so early in our relationship, but I'm sure you will also understand that very few things in this life come free, and there will be a price to pay for the luxury which awaits us.' His dark, expressive eyes held her alert face in their aspect.

Was this it? she wondered. Was he about to admit that he had married her as a matter of convenience and to tell her why? No. Almost immediately she discounted the idea, for hadn't he said that such an admission would hardly be in his own interests?

She shrugged her silk-clad shoulders. 'That sounds rather boring. I do hope it doesn't include me.'

'Unfortunately it does, but I'm sure it won't stretch your capabilities too much.' There was the slightest hint of asperity in his tone and she thought she saw a brief flash of irritation in his level glance. Good, she determined. Already Nicolò was finding out that she wasn't the compliant idiot for which he had taken her! 'Tonight I have to host a presentation and reception given for the Press and many of our clients from Europe and the States—that is what Giovanni meant by "guests". I had hoped to introduce you to the *palazzo* at leisure, to share the afternoon with you...'

He didn't expand his meaning, but Catia had no need of a translation. His intentions were written in the sudden passionate intensity of his eyes as they dwelt on her face with obvious sexual hunger. 'Unfortunately——' he shrugged lazy shoulders '—the flight delay has meant we have just enough time to get ourselves ready to greet our guests, and we will have to wait until we have seen the last one off the premises before we can truly be alone together. Do you mind too much?'

So despite his lack of love for her he didn't intend their marriage to be platonic! The realisation both frightened and appalled her. With every cell of her body aware of his nearness, her heart fluttering like a humming-bird's wings, her mouth damp with the expectation of tasting him, she had to force herself to remember that he didn't love her, that his masquerade of passionate bridegroom was a sham.

At the very most all he was portraying was the normal healthy appetite of an adult male who was very sure of his ground. Far from being disappointed, in the circumstances she was relieved! Every minute she could distance herself from his powerful charisma, the more time she would gain to arm herself mentally and emotionally against him.

'Of course not; I love parties!' She forced excitement into her voice as a plan began to take place in her tortured mind. She could make him believe that she had agreed to marry him because of his wealth, that she had never had any real feelings for him. By attacking his masculine pride she might be able to keep him out of her bed, and preserve the remnants of her self-esteem until she'd found out why he had deceived her. When she knew the truth she would be better armed to extricate herself from this impossible position.

'*Dio*!' The huskiness of his voice was oddly alarming as he responded to her sang-froid. 'Is this an example of your English phlegm? It would have been more flattering to pretend devastation at the idea rather than resignation!'

Even then, she was only half prepared for the powerful fervency of his embrace as he took her into his arms, only partially ready to receive the hot thrust of his tongue as it claimed her mouth as his own. As if she had been plugged into the mains electricity supply her whole body became transformed, trembling with a need which refused to be subjected to her iron self-control.

With dismay she realised that although her mind had rejected him and all he stood for her body had yet to be taught the same lesson. She had indeed stung his male pride, but instead of retreating he had extorted payment for such an insult, springing on her when she'd been totally unprepared for his punitive action, and there was nothing she could do but suffer in silence.

'*Santo cielo*!' He broke the embrace minutes later, releasing her mouth to utter the exclamation at the same time as he eased his aroused body away from her. 'Do you want to be deflowered on the public highway?'

Despite her own tormented feelings, his expression of mixed agony, despair and doleful acceptance of his predicament brought a pale smile to Catia's lips, as well as a surge of triumph to her heart. He had treated her and her grandfather appallingly. Frustrating him would be a small revenge for what he had done to her, and a temporary one too, she was sure. A man of Nicolò Cacciatore's undoubted sexual magnetism wouldn't stay frustrated for long. But at least, she determined grimly, he would realise he wasn't irresistible to every woman.

'Don't you mean canalway?' she enquired sweetly, stroking her hair into place as if the only emotion she was experiencing was mild irritation that it had been disarranged.

'Highway—seaway—canalway.' He glowered at her, whether in annoyance or mock-despair she couldn't be certain. 'In Venice it is all the same thing.' Fingers which only showed the slightest tremor swept through his close-clinging cap of dark hair. 'Come!' he instructed with a touch of the old autocratic manner which was always there beneath the veneer of charm which typified his personality as she knew it. 'We have already entered the Grand Canal and soon we shall be passing the Basilica San Marco. It is a sight not to be missed, especially as the sun begins to set.'

'*Perfetta*! *Squisita*!' Three hours later Nicolò rewarded the pains Catia had taken with her appearance by according her his approval. 'The prospect of being the centre of attention has certainly brought a sparkle to your beautiful eyes.'

'Of course!' She glanced at the nearby mirror, congratulating herself on the way she was managing to hide her turbulent emotions from Nicolò's dissecting gaze. It was an effort to portray the kind of character she'd decided to adopt without overplaying her hand and arousing his suspicions, but she thought she was doing quite well. Amid the pain which racked her heart was a feeling of anticipation as to how he would react as she revealed the 'new' Caterina Laurence in all her petulant glory! With a bit of luck he would acknowledge how great was the mistake he'd made and take steps to annul their unholy union. No, she corrected herself silently, with a lot of luck! Because until she discovered his true motives in arranging this liaison she was unable to judge the importance of the role she had been called upon to fill.

'I'm looking forward to it,' she lied, eyeing her image in the mirror, feigning pleasure at her reflection. 'It will be like having another wedding reception, except, of course, no one will know I'm the bride!'

'Ah, now there you are wrong, *mia cara*,' Nicolò told her softly. 'You will find that I am not without some fame here in Venice, and already it is widely known that I have forsaken my bachelordom for the love of a beautiful foreigner. Even if people don't immediately guess your identity, despite the fact that I am renowned for my taste for beauty, once I have introduced you to a few intimates the whole room will be buzzing with the knowledge.'

'Let's hope they won't be disappointed . . .' She put an edge of petulance to her voice as she fingered the flame silk of her dress, dismissing his overt flattery for the little it was worth. 'If you'd forewarned me I would have bought something expensive in London before leaving, instead of waiting to restock my wardrobe here in Italy. Something more fitted to the wife of a wealthy man.'

'Really?' She hadn't expected the blank, shuttered expression with which he confronted her. 'And there was I believing that you chose to wear that dress specially tonight because it brought back happy memories.'

Oh, dear heavens! That was a blow beneath the belt. She'd bought the orange-red silk chiffon dress in a sale at a fashionable boutique in London's New Bond Street, priding herself in obtaining such a well-cut garment at such a low price. The boat-shaped neckline with its gently draping folds was a perfect foil for her honey-coloured skin, while the waistline settled easily against her own slim middle before the skirt swirled out into soft folds at mid-calf level.

She'd worn it to a dinner dance hosted by Richard Carville on behalf of a racing syndicate for which he was the bloodstock adviser. It had been during her first week back at Suddingham, and of course Nicolò had been there.

They'd danced together and it had been the first time he'd held her so closely. She'd hardly drunk any alcohol, but she'd felt light-headed: disorientated but not afraid. Like a moth being drawn towards the candle which would scorch it to extinction, she'd seemed to possess no will-power which would enable her to detach herself from the powerful magnetism of the man whose aura dominated her own. In retrospect she realised she had already begun on the downward path which had spiralled to this, her final humiliation. Now he was laughing at her vulnerability, taunting her with her weakness.

'It was all right for Suddingham.' She made a move of disapproval, deciding to ignore his bait. 'But now I'm in Venice I want to restock my wardrobe with designer labels.'

'Never judge quality by price, Catia *mia*,' Nicolò rebuked her lightly. 'Your natural taste is excellent, and, even if it were not so, your loveliness would outshine even a fashion disaster.' He took a step backwards and surveyed her from head to toe with a discerning eye. 'No earrings tonight?'

She shook her head, surprised that he'd seemed to remember her predilection for such trinkets. Tonight she'd thought costume jewellery might be a little out of place in the opulence of her surroundings, and had preferred to leave her ears unadorned, but Nicolò had given her another opportunity to act the shrew, and it was one she was quick to seize.

'I've nothing suitable,' she declared captiously. 'How can I wear simulated stones when all the other women will be wearing real ones? It would reflect very badly on you, wouldn't it?'

Nicolò's strong mouth pursed for a moment as a shadow flickered across his eyes, then he was sliding one hand inside the immaculately cut jacket of his evening suit. 'Then you will not be disappointed with these, I think.'

The thin black leather case he offered her opened at her fingers' pressure to reveal a necklet of gold made from overlapping segments like the scales of a fish. Nestled within its circle and gleaming on the white satin lining were long, dangling matching earrings. Her mouth opened in silent awe as instinctively she recognised the superb creation of a Venetian designer—eye-catching without vulgarity, hideously expensive but without plebeian showiness.

'No need to thank me now.' Nicolò dismissed her speechlessness with an ironic twist of his mouth. 'As you say, it would reflect very badly on my generosity if you were unable to compete with the other women present. Besides, I can wait until tonight for you to find the words and actions to express your gratitude. Here—allow me...'

Taking the box and contents from her unprotesting hands, he removed the latter before tossing the former on to the elegant dressing-table of the large double bedroom into which he had ushered her after allowing her a quick look around the ground-floor ballroom.

Standing motionless, she allowed him to fasten the necklace into place, hearing his soft grunt of approval as it nestled against her skin. But when she felt the soft clasp of the earrings embrace her small lobes she turned towards him in surprise.

'How clever of you to find earrings with clips,' she exclaimed, masking her instinctive pleasure at such craftsmanship as she forced herself to preen before the mirror. 'Most expensive earrings are made for pierced ears only, and mine aren't!'

'Did you think I was not aware of every inch of your lovely body which is exposed to public gaze, hmm?' he riposted, his expression enigmatic as she fingered the loop of gold around her neck. 'Or that I would scour the shops of Venice for what I wanted? No, *dolce mia*, no other woman in the *palazzo* tonight will wear a duplicate of these pretty trinkets. They were designed specifically for you and to my instructions.'

'You ordered them when you came back to Venice after I'd accepted your proposal?' she hazarded, suppressing a shiver. What had he in store for her if he was prepared to make such payment in advance for her services?

His dark head shook, dismissing the notion. 'Craftsmen of the quality of Mario Principe need time to produce their best. I placed my order with him the day after I first met you.'

'Truly?' Catia's hand rose to her throat, the glistening gold cold against her warm fingers, as a feeling of faintness washed over her. Had his strength of purpose really been as positive and unrelenting as that? There was something frightening about being hunted down with such steely determination. He'd always meant to tear her away from her grandfather by fair means or foul—every action he'd taken proclaimed it—and poor Nonno had been powerless to resist him. Was it revenge? her fevered brain wondered. Revenge against Nonno for some previous wrong? To deprive him of the thing he held most dear—herself? She had read of such things but never imagined the kind of man who would saddle himself with an unwanted companion out of spite alone.

'*Davvero*!' Nicolò interrupted her chain of thought, confirming the accuracy of her question, as a cool hauteur tightened the strong lines of his face. 'I had intended for you to wear it at our wedding—and so you shall. Our real wedding, not the civil farce which sufficed as such this morning. Tomorrow we will hire a designer to make you a wedding-dress which will be a suitable foil to your English-rose beauty and my gift to you.'

'Nicolò . . .' Anguish echoed in her spontaneous use of his name. There was something about the set of his profile as he made to turn away that intensified her uneasiness, as much as the reminder that it was his intention to bind her to him with even stronger ties, something she must resist with all her might.

'Yes?' He paused, his dark eyes travelling over her pale face. 'Something is troubling you?'

'No, not really.' She shrugged off his concern. It was too early to reveal her hand. There was still so much she didn't know. All she could do was play for time and hope that she would soon get an insight into Nicolò's dark purpose. There had to be some advantage he would gain by his masquerade. Given time, she would discover it—and, if it was within her power, thwart it!

But he was still waiting, his brows drawn together, watching her with an air of disquiet, so that she was forced to find an explanation for her interruption.

'I was just wondering if Nonno's condition that we should have a civil marriage before leaving England caused you a great deal of trouble,' she improvised airily, gathering all her sorely tried resources together.

'No.' The terse monosyllable denied her supposition. 'If I had a granddaughter as desirable as you, I, too, would have insisted that she was legally married before entrusting her to a *contadino* like myself. Besides, it gave you the opportunity of inviting all your friends to witness our happiness and share our celebration. I doubt, even if we had paid their fares, whether many of them could have found the time to travel to Venice for the church ceremony which will give us God's blessing as well as that of the state. I'm sorry I had to take you away from the reception so early, but I imagine the fun went on without us.'

'Yes, I'm sure it did.' She failed to hide the bitterness in her voice. All fun had ended for her in one traumatic moment. At least Nicolò had spoken one word of truth to her when he had referred to himself as a *contadino*. For all his obvious wealth, he was as morally bankrupt as the peasant he had nominated himself as was financially!

'Regrets already?' With a sudden movement he was in front of her, tipping up her chin with steely fingers, his dark eyes searching her expression challengingly, attempting to read her emotions as if they were written in large print across her forehead.

'Of course not!' she protested querulously, a sense of imminent danger warning her to conceal her hand. 'How could I ever regret becoming your wife, Nicolò?'

She'd intended the reply to sound rhetorical, but at the last moment her hidden pain manifested itself so that her words sounded contentious.

'I don't know, Caterina.' Nicolò's quiet answer sent a spasm of apprehension down her spine, as she became unbearably aware of the closeness of his very male body. 'But I warn you against it, because I shall never let you go. What I have I hold. And after the church ceremony we shall be bound by stronger ties than those of man alone!'

Closing her eyes, she blotted out his face, terrifyingly aware that his physical power over her was still as strong as it had been when she'd loved him. But that was absurd! How could she desire a man who had done both her and her grandfather such disservice?

She uttered a small cry of resistance as his hands left her face to draw her body into the close, passionate embrace of a lover. Shuddering beneath the caressing sweep of his fingers, she was powerless to escape the possessive intensity of his lips. Her senses assaulted her as his sweetly searching tongue found sanctuary in the warm darkness of her mouth; to her dismay she experienced the reawakening of the savage physical hunger which had blinded her to his deception.

Shaking when he released her, she was aware she had received a warning as much as a promise of his future intentions. Their marriage might have been arranged, but he intended to enjoy every right accorded to a husband in common and divine law.

'Do I make myself clear?' He was still too close for comfort. Near enough to see the pulse trembling in her throat, to hear her swift breathing, to perceive the musky scent of her sudden fear. She should be congratulating herself that she'd managed to get beneath his skin with her subtle change of character. She'd supposed it would take some time to make him aware that she was no longer the docile bride he had taken, but she'd obviously underestimated his sensibility. Her triumph was muted by the realisation that she was playing with a fire more dangerous than she'd first assessed.

One thing was certain. Whatever happened, she must prevent the church wedding from taking place. Until it did, she had an escape route. Not an easy one, it was true, but easier than if she was forced into undergoing the full panoply of a church wedding here in Venice.

'Caterina?' Nicolò spoke her name as if it were a question. 'I'm waiting for your answer.'

She'd seen only the smooth, graceful side of his nature in England. On his own ground his natural arrogance was stunning. Her pulse-beat heightened in intensity, as his dark eyes demanded her compliance.

'For heaven's sake...' She forced herself to trivialise the situation by inducing a note of peevishness into her voice as she reached for a tissue to touch her lips with a careless insolence that registered in the sudden frown on Nicolò's face. 'Aren't I entitled to be a little upset after the dreadful journey we had? Do you have to make such a large production number just because I'm tired and now face the ordeal of meeting a lot of strange people, knowing that I shall be the worst-dressed woman there?'

'Is that all it is?' His mouth twisted into the smile that had once flipped her heart. 'Forgive me, *cara mia*. For a moment I thought I had married your twin sister by mistake; I saw so little of the woman who'd stood beside me this morning and pledged her life to mine. But now I know that it is frustration and thwarted vanity which brings the colour to your cheeks and the sharpness to your voice, I understand. But be assured, you underestimate the impact of your appearance on my guests. Shall we go downstairs, and check that everything is as it should be for their entertainment?'

He made it sound like a question, but the way he took her with him from the bedroom towards the sweeping staircase which led downwards to the grand reception hall of the *palazzo* left no time for her to demur. Not that she wanted to, Catia accorded. For the time being she was Caterina Cacciatore, the wife of Nicolò Cacciatore, and she would play out that role until such time as she discovered what lay behind it, and devised a way to exit from this agony.

The unexpected party had provided her with time to ponder on and evaluate her situation, to try to eradicate the feelings she still, incredibly, nurtured for Nicolò in the light of the truth she had discovered. And what of tonight, when the party was over and they returned to the marital bedroom? It was incredible to remember that only hours earlier she had been anticipating the night with a joyous expectation, convinced that Nicolò would make her first experience of total lovemaking an unforgettable occasion.

If only she could believe that he intended to leave her alone, but such self-deception was impossible. She shivered. When the time came for them to retire she would find an excuse not to consummate their union, that night or any other night. Whatever his sins, surely Nicolò wouldn't take her against her will? And it would be against her will, she accorded fiercely, because the shock of discovering his duplicity had killed any last vestige of love she had had for Nicolò Cacciatore. All that was left was the imprint of a dangerous and soul-destroying fantasy.

CHAPTER THREE

IT WAS one o'clock the following morning when Catia made an unobtrusive exit from the ballroom, leaving behind the glistening chandeliers, the deep red velvet curtains with their golden sashes, and the hum of voices to seek sanctuary in the adjacent garden.

From inside the *palazzo* came the sound of music and laughter. Outside the air was cool, sweetly scented with the perfume of flowering privet. As the launch had turned into the minor canal which flowed alongside the *palazzo* and moored against the small landing-stage, she had caught a glimpse of overhanging trees, of baskets of flowers strung across the slender iron rails of a balcony. She had anticipated a patio where she might enjoy the open air, gain a temporary respite from the overwhelming weight of despair which haunted her, but the reality exceeded her expectations.

Dim lights cleverly placed in foliage revealed not only the open space she had hoped for, but secluded corners where vines crept across trellis and slender saplings rustled in the night breeze. As her eyes grew used to the subdued lighting she realised that the scent of privet came from a row of shrubs carefully pruned to become small standards, set in containers around a raised bed of Chinese hibiscus, the latter's tightly furled spent blossoms deep orange against the dark green lustre of their leaves.

But it was the white stone balustrade overlooking the Grand Canal which compelled her attention. Carved into its sweeping curves was a long seat covered in a deep-filled cushion. Kneeling on its softness, her arms resting on the wide coping, Catia stared eagerly into the starlit night, temporarily divorcing her mind from its turmoil. Lights from a nearby hotel revealed a row of gondolas tied to their black and red striped posts, their domed lamps gleaming, moving gently on the swell. In the distance on the opposite bank she could just make out the awesome silhouette of the cupolas belonging to the baroque Basilica of Santa Maria della Salute, the seventeenth-century church built to celebrate the departure of the plague from the city.

She yawned suddenly, covering her mouth with the palm of her hand, although there was no one present to witness the action. Eighteen hours had passed since she'd risen from her bed the previous morning, she realised with a small start of surprise, during which time she had become a married woman, drunk her fill of champagne, discovered she'd been cruelly deceived, flown across Europe, put on a brave face while she attended a glittering presentation in her husband's *palazzo*, and shaken hands with too many people to be able to make a head-count.

Doubtless she'd been kept going by the force of her own adrenalin, but now, in the peace and stillness of the garden, she felt a surge of tiredness, welcoming its onset, because it would give her the excuse to repel any attempt at so-called lovemaking by Nicolò. There would be no satisfaction for him in bedding an exhausted woman and she prayed he wouldn't insist on his rights in the face of her sustained lethargy, however deep his annoyance.

'Ah, *che bella fortuna*! I find you enjoying the night air by yourself, Marchesa!'

At the sound of the pleasant male voice close behind her Catia swivelled round on her perch, rising to her feet, a slight frown marring the pale perfection of her forehead. *How* had he addressed her?

'Allow me to introduce myself. . . Cesare Brunelli—at your service, Marchesa.'

Lithe and slender, only a few inches taller than her own five feet six inches, Catia judged him to be in his late twenties. He was a personable young man with a wide, thin-lipped mouth and the bright eyes of an inquisitive monkey, attired in a well-fitting evening suit.

'Signor Brunelli, I am delighted to meet you.' Forcing herself to be polite, Catia took the hand which was extended to her in greeting, and a flicker of a smile crossed her lips as her own hand was raised to the stranger's lips and lightly brushed in formal politeness. 'But I'm afraid I'm not who you believe me to be. I'm the wife of Nicolò Cacciatore—not a *marchesa*.'

'Caterina Cacciatore.' Cesare Brunelli's dark head dipped to acknowledge her protest, but with no appearance of discomfiture. 'Perhaps the way I addressed you was a little premature, but in the fullness of time—no? If I have offended you by anticipating the future, then I beg your pardon.'

'No, I'm not at all offended, just puzzled.' Catia's brain was working overtime to make sense of what she had just heard. The apology might have sounded innocent, but there was something about the young man's attitude, a wariness allied to deliberation, which suggested his artlessness was assumed. Her frown returned, deepening as an explanation struck her. An explanation that bordered on the incredible! 'Are you telling me that Nicolò, my husband, is in line to inherit the title of Marchese?' she exclaimed.

'Cacciatore?' Her companion's brows rose in well-modulated astonishment. 'Good heavens, no! Nicolò Cacciatore comes from a long line of undistinguished peasants whose forebears scraped a living by raising cattle on the hills of Calabria.' He gave a snort of amusement which brought the colour flooding to her face.

'If that is so, then his achievements are worth even greater acclaim!' she remonstrated sharply, then wondered why she had felt it necessary to fly to Nicolò's defence.

'Perhaps.' The sleek dark head nodded, the thin lips pursed. 'On the other hand, by the time his father had forsaken meat-on-the-hoof to invest in meat-between-two-pieces-of-bread, by starting his own fast-food chain, the family fortunes had improved almost beyond belief. No——' he turned slightly, raising his gaze to encompass the dull ochre-painted walls of the *palazzo* as they rose to meet the night sky '—the Cacciatore family are not short of money or anything it can buy. What they lack is the nobility to match their pretensions!'

Somewhere deep inside her Catia felt a flicker of interest spring to life. 'You presume a lot, to insult my husband in his own house,' she said carefully, conscious that she should not appear too eager for information until she knew whether it would be of assistance to her. 'I don't know who you are——'

'Cesare Brunelli.' He bowed. 'I forgive you for not remembering. Today has been a day full of new faces and new names, and, despite your heritage, Italian is not your first language, is it? But since when has the truth been an insult, Marchesa?'

'Since *you* allied it to your own interpretation, *signore*.' She paused, as if awaiting an apology which didn't come. 'I think perhaps it's time I rejoined the party.' She went to move away, hoping that her appearance of uninterest would lure him to further revelations. But before he could speak again one of her high heels skidded on the uneven surface of the stone beneath them, forcing her to stop with a small yelp of pain.

'Are you hurt, Marchesa?' Instantly Cesare Brunelli was in front of her. To aid her or to bar her way?

'No, *grazie*.' The small word of thanks was curt, dismissive, but he stayed firmly where he was, one hand supporting her arm. 'And please don't call me by that absurd title!'

She felt his hand tighten on her elbow, restraining her. 'What else should I call the granddaughter of a *marchese*?' he asked softly.

'What did you say?' Low-spirited though she was Catia couldn't prevent the small cascade of laughter which left her parted lips. 'Nonno? A *marchese*? Now I know you're either mad or drunk!'

'So you really didn't know,' Cesare Brunelli said softly, his hand dropping from her arm. 'I can understand why Cacciatore would want to keep it a secret until after he had captured you as his wife, but what persuasion could he have used to persuade your grandfather to be so reticent, hmm?' he mused. 'And why are you still in ignorance?'

She should go, should leave him alone with his fantasies, since they were of no help to her, but something intangible froze her where she stood. 'Because the whole absurd idea is a figment of your imagination,' she answered wearily.

'No.' Just the monosyllable, quiet and authoritative. 'No. It is the truth. I, Cesare Brunelli, can vouch for that... Antonio Lorenzo, Marchese di Castellone. It took the Italian lawyers a long, long time to trace him when the old Marchese died. No close heirs, just a distant cousin who had seemingly disappeared into thin air, but who was eventually traced to a small English village.' He smiled, revealing the white teeth of a predator. 'Antonio Lorenzo, heir to the Marchese di Castellone, a bankrupt estate in Tuscany, and a handful of debts. Antonio Lorenzo—and his beautiful, unmarried granddaughter...the future Marchesa... The jewel of nobility for the commercial crown of Cacciatore!'

There was no denying the ring of truth in his voice. It sent a shiver down her back as her hands crossed to caress her upper arms, calming their trembling. Could it really be as simple and as terrible as that? She had to make certain, because if it was it explained a great deal.

'If what you say is true, Signor Brunelli——' she began carefully.

'Cesare, please, Marchesa; everybody calls me Cesare.'

Ignoring his interjection, Catia continued stoically, 'I can tell you categorically that my grandfather knows nothing of it.'

'And I can tell you that if you truly believe that then you have been misled,' her tormentor responded crisply. 'I have excellent contacts in the legal firm which instituted the search for the successor to the title. It was an interesting little problem which intrigued me and one which I thought would amuse my readers once it was solved, and so it proved. The successful result of the search was syndicated in my column all over Italy.'

'You're a reporter?' A strange feeling of light-headedness was creeping over her. 'A reporter, here at the *palazzo*?'

Cesare Brunelli inclined his head. 'I prefer the label "*journalist*," since I do not run with a pack but discover and follow up my own stories. And here? Of course, why not? The social columns are as important as the motoring desk in promotions such as your husband has hosted tonight. Like it or not, *signora*, I am here by invitation.'

Why in heaven's name hadn't her grandfather told her? The answer sprang immediately to her troubled mind. Because Nicolò had forbidden him to do so. Nicolò had never intended her to discover the reason for his amorous pursuit until it was too late for her to escape. But, thanks to what she'd overheard and the confirmation she'd just received, he had failed. Nicolò could do what he would, but he'd never be able to drag her to the altar now unless he drugged her first! A civil union was bad enough, but at least it would be easier to break than a moral one.

'You seem distressed, Marchesa.' Brunelli's light voice weaved itself into her consciousness, as he made an expansive gesture with his right hand. 'Forgive me, I do you a great disservice even to suggest that it was the title rather than you that he lusted after. Nicolò Cacciatore has always been a great connoisseur of the female sex. I was foolish to suppose for a moment it was anything other than your beauty which attracted him to your side.'

He smiled, but his eyes were watchful, as he added casually, 'I, for one, was never fooled by the rumours that he was passionately in love with Gina Cabrini and that they were planning to set up house together if she could free herself legally from her husband without creating a scandal which would rock the Cacciatore empire. Everyone knows that Giuseppe Cabrini is hardly likely to be so indiscreet as to give her the ammunition she seeks.'

'Gina Cabrini?' She should have kept her mouth closed, but the name slipped between cold lips, as she faced up to another facet of Nicolò's deception. Cesare Brunelli could hardly know she had already discovered she'd been tricked into marrying Nicolò, and she could see quite clearly what he was doing—denying what he assumed to be the truth as a kind of bait to lure her to indiscretion.

Suddenly she was aware of movement in the minor canal beside the entrance: launches arriving, the sound of voices. People were leaving and she should put in a reappearance, play the dutiful wife until it pleased her to show her hand.

'Your husband hasn't mentioned the exotic Gina?' Still at her side, her tormentor parodied amazement. 'What an omission! Everybody who is anybody in Venezia knows Gina! She's one of the city's most famous daughters, owning a chain of fashion boutiques throughout France and Italy.' He pursed his lips as if considering a point. 'There are many who will tell you that she spent too much time with her business and not enough with her husband, and that is why the marriage failed. Others...' He shrugged his shoulders. 'Well, others will tell you that Giuseppe Cabrini discovered his wife had been unfaithful and, although he suspected who her lover was, he couldn't prove it...'

'I think you've said enough.' Anger at his temerity momentarily overcame Catia's desire to hear the whole painful scenario. The sudden ache in her chest as her diaphragm tightened made breathing difficult for her and she raised her palm to her breast, feeling the fast beating of her heart. An arch manipulator, Nicolò had achieved two objects by making her his wife. Their marriage would be a screen behind which he and his lover could conceal themselves, at the same time providing a link with the so-called nobility of old Italy which Nicolò's pagan heart lusted after. A lonely voice wailed inside her. Oh, Nicolò, how could you be so wicked . . . ? 'My husband——' she began painfully.

'Your husband? Did I suggest that he is Gina's lover?' Dark eyebrows rose in simulated astonishment. 'You misjudge me, Marchesa. If that were the case he would hardly have married you, would he? Unless, of course, he had wanted to throw Cabrini off the track. Rumours say that each is searching for evidence against the other so that their separation may be turned into a divorce. Imagine the scandal! It would certainly have been an embarrassment if Cacciatore had been the guilty party, because Cabrini is the financial director of your husband's company . . .'

She hadn't needed Brunelli's succinct summing-up of her predicament. The *modus operandi* was quite clear. Not only had the old Marchese's death led to her grandfather's whereabouts being publicly revealed, thus exposing him to collection of the debt he'd owed the Cacciatore family, but it had made the debt worth collecting in the shape of herself. And if her grandfather had shown reluctance to see her suborned into a loveless marriage Nicolò would, doubtless, have been able to sweeten the deal by offering to settle the old Marchese's financial debts into the bargain. Perhaps he'd already done so when he'd broached the subject with Nonno? That would explain the mention of a debt between them. A small price to pay for the advantages Nicolò stood to gain.

Damn him, she thought as anger flushed her cheeks. How dared he treat her with such total arrogance? He must have played his hand with great care to gain her grandfather's agreement, using his golden tongue to persuade the old man that her destiny lay in Italy, the country of her ancestors, because Nonno would never have agreed to the union for financial benefit alone, would he?

Without another word she thrust herself past the smirking Italian. Let him think his stories had fallen on deaf ears. If only he knew how grateful she was for his malicious gossip he wouldn't be so satisfied with himself, she opined.

The ballroom was emptying fast, the members of the small orchestra packing their instruments away. Aware that she was still breathing heavily, she paused just inside the threshold of the beautiful room, clutching at one of the heavy drapes for support, staring sightlessly at the magnificently restored floor. She had wanted to discover the facts. Why was she feeling so devastated? Could it have been that all the time she had been praying that by some miracle she had mistaken the conversation in her grandfather's study? That Nicolò really did love her as deeply as she loved him? *Had* loved him, she corrected. Sharply she chastised herself. She was old enough to know that miracles were not a part of twentieth-century life.

'Catia—where have you been?' Nicolò's voice sounding sharply in her ear brought her eyes up to focus on his stern face. 'I was worried about you.'

'You thought I'd run away, deserted you on our wedding night?' There was a trace of hysteria in her laugh. 'Why would I want to do that?'

'You're unwell.' It was a statement, as dark eyes appraised her dispassionately, dismissing her attempt at levity. 'You have been acting strangely ever since we set foot in Italy. What's wrong, *carissima*?'

She flinched at the sound of the easy but insincere endearment. 'I'm tired,' she told him flatly, resolutely dismissing the note of concern in Nicolò's voice as play-acting. 'The whole evening's been a bit of a bore. I didn't realise how dull it would be!'

'*Povera piccola . . .*' Nicolò's palm grazed her cheek, and she started away from it as if she'd been stung. 'This is not the way we should have spent our first evening together as man and wife. You are as pale as a Bellini Madonna. Come, the party is nearly over. I'll take you up to our apartment and rejoin you as soon as I am able.'

Dumbly Catia nodded. There was no point in defying him, even if she had so wished. She could tell from his expression that if she had demurred he would have swept her up into his arms and forcibly transferred her.

As it was he merely supported her with his arm around her waist as they mounted the marble-faced staircase and entered the wide vestibule from which the various apartments were reached. Vaguely she was aware of the rich Turkish rugs strewn beneath her feet, knew that they were old and therefore very valuable. Somewhere she had read that the worst thing one could do was display a Turkish rug on the wall, because its true value came from wear, the passage of feet tightening the thousands of hand-tied knots and enhancing the quality.

'Go to bed, Catia.' To her great relief Nicolò made no attempt to kiss her as he ushered her over the threshold of their bedroom. 'You have had a tiring day. I will join you as soon as I can.'

Alone in the room, she collapsed on to the bed, her mind racing as her eyes wandered round her surroundings, seeing but not registering the fitted carpet the soft colour of an unripe almond shell, the half-panelled walls displaying a variety of paintings, the high ceiling with its intricate plasterwork. Nervously her hands fingered the cover of the king-size bed.

Nausea ached behind her ribs at the realisation of what she would have to face when Nicolò returned, and she refused to accommodate his desires. Wearily she rose from the bed. Suppose he refused her plea of exhaustion? During their brief engagement he'd tempered his desire on the few opportunities they'd been together out of respect for her grandfather's ideals and her own wish to keep faith with the mores of her upbringing, or at least that was what she'd supposed. Now she saw his reticence to alienate her in an entirely different light.

In retrospect she could only rejoice that her somewhat old-fashioned views had prevented her from making the mistake of encouraging him to become her lover. As it was, her pride, her dignity and her resolution never to let him conquer her spirit were still intact!

Carefully, with fingers which trembled, she removed the jewellery which had been Nicolò's gift and placed it in the presentation box before disrobing completely and entering the *en-suite* bathroom, carrying her nightdress with her. Hoping that the brief warm shower she took would revive her, she was disappointed to find that it was ineffective.

Like a zombie she went through the motions, drying herself and smoothing her favourite body lotion which matched her perfume into her soft honey skin before slipping her nightdress over her head. In an automatic gesture she smoothed the folds of the ice-blue heavy satin garment over her slenderly rounded hips. It was more like a ball-gown than a nightdress, with its figure-hugging top and full-length flowing skirt, and she had purchased it in joyful anticipation of the first time she would wear it. Where now was that exhilaration she had envisaged?

The silent bedroom awaited her, as noiselessly she made her way to the bed, pulling back the cover to reveal silk sheets patterned in shades of pale blue and grey with a plain wide toning binding, and matching pillowslips; she was scarcely aware of their luxury as she eased her tired body between them.

Sleep; she needed sleep. It was an impossible urge to resist. As her hand raised to switch off the bedside lamp, her last thought was that Nicolò would have to awaken her before he could claim the rights that he would doubtless expect to be his.

It was barely light when she awakened. For a moment she supposed she was alone in the vast bed. Drawing herself into a sitting position, she discovered her mistake. Beside her, separated by the width of another person, Nicolò's peaceful profile dented the multi-coloured pillowcase, while the fully exposed length of his naked golden torso, its muscled strength relaxed in slumber, made the breath catch in her throat.

Even as she wondered at his restraint the previous night, memories of her encounter with Cesare Brunelli flooded back into her mind. The deep sleep of exhaustion had repaired her body tissues and sharpened her brain, so now she was prepared to continue the part she had decided to play.

Carefully, she swung her legs out of bed, gathering a collection of casual clothes in the dim light and taking them into the bathroom with her. It took but a few minutes to wash, clean her teeth and dress in jeans, T-shirt and light jacket. She needed more time to work out her strategy, and for that she wanted to be alone.

Leaving the bedroom without disturbing Nicolò, she made her way downstairs, through the deserted ballroom, and slid aside one of the glass doors leading to the garden. Last night she'd noticed a wrought-iron gate leading to the landing-stage at the side of the *palazzo*. It took seconds to slide the bolts, lift the latch and make her way across the decorative stone bridge which crossed the minor canal.

Her casual leather slip-ons making no sound, she hurried towards the maze of streets which she knew, from the journey the previous day, would lead her towards the dominating Piazza di San Marco. Leaving the Grand Canal, wreathed in early morning mist, behind her, she knew as long as she remembered where it lay in respect to the direction she took she would be able to retrace her steps.

Wandering through the narrow, deserted streets, with their useful yellow plaques giving directions to San Marco or the Rialto Bridge, she crossed silent squares where pigeons bathed in the pools of water left by dripping pumps, hardly aware of the balconies with their masses of flowers or the honeysuckle vines which covered softly coloured walls. Venice was only just beginning to stir in response to another dawn, and she was able to relive the previous night's revelations in the solitude she needed.

She shuddered as she considered the part Cesare Brunelli had played. One of nature's vultures who sat on the fence waiting for the carrion to feast on and grow fat, Brunelli didn't have to be liked or respected to be believed. His motives were clear. He wanted to stir up more scandal for his columns. He had no personal animosity towards either her or Nicolò, but neither had he any conscience as to the results of his actions.

Her eyes blurred by tears, she paused as her feet led her to a narrow bridge spanning a minor canal. Blinking rapidly, she allowed her gaze to linger on the deep, still reflection of the tall surrounding houses, which turned the water to a glimmering sheet of shot silk as the sun's rays finally pierced the haze. A small boat lay motionless against its mooring, and geraniums tumbled down a soft pink wall, its surface crumbling and peeling. A bright blue plastic bucket made an incongruous splash of harsh colour against the softness of the surrounding masonry and in the distance she could see the perfectly formed reflection of the next bridge, while her own world crumbled in fragments around her.

Her hands tightened on the handrail of the bridge. Her fate was in her own hands, but she must be subtle. Instinctively she knew that dircct confrontation would not be to her advantage. But one way or another she determined she would force Nicolò Cacciatore to acknowledge just how great a mistake he had made, and persuade him that it was in both their best interests to set her free.

CHAPTER FOUR

'WHERE have you been?'

Distracted by her thoughts, Catia had taken several wrong turnings before eventually discovering her way back to the *palazzo*, to find herself face-to-face with a furious Nicolò as she crossed the bridge and re-entered the grounds. Expression thunderous, his voice controlled but edged with anger, he seized her roughly by the arms.

Alarm quickened the beat of her heart. At last he was about to show his true colours, exert his authority over her. Suddenly her mouth was dry.

'For a walk,' she returned with assumed calm, casting a haughty glance at the lean fingers imprisoning her, although her heart continued its rapid tattoo. 'Surely that's not a crime? I awakened early and couldn't get back to sleep again. I wanted something to do.'

'And it didn't occur to you that if you'd awakened me I could have found something for *both* of us to do?' The suggestive gleam in his dark eyes left her in no doubt of his meaning.

On the point of retorting that it was *because* she had realised precisely what he would have found to do if she had awakened him, Catia took refuge in caution. 'You appeared to be fast asleep and I didn't want to disturb you. After all, I had no idea what time you came to bed.'

'Not long after I'd seen you to our room.' Dark lashes masked the expression of his unblinking regard. 'Is this what all this is about? Because I didn't wake you up to exercise the rights and privileges of a husband? Did you feel neglected, *mio tesoro*, and decide that I should pay for my negligence by putting the fear of God into me?'

'Fear?' Her startled gaze betrayed her surprise. 'What was there to fear? Surely Venice is one of the safest cities in the world?'

'Yes.' His fingers curled possessively around her arms. 'It is what we like to believe, but, faced with the sudden disappearance of his bride, a man may be forgiven for imagining the worst.'

'You thought I'd been kidnapped?' Catia's laugh was incredulous. 'All I wanted to do was to explore the heart of Venice.'

'While I had quite a different kind of exploration in mind for you,' Nicolò said drily. 'And one which would be more properly conducted in the privacy of our own apartment than here on the mooring-bay where inquisitive eyes may detect us. Come!'

Resigned to face the battle which lay ahead, Catia allowed herself to be urged towards the garden entrance. Nicolò had to be taught that she was no chattel to be used to promote a man's business and provide a screen for an illicit love-affair. He would have to learn that the pride of a Lorenzo equalled that of a Cacciatore, although teaching him might not be without its own peril!

A team of servants intent on cleaning and polishing the ballroom floor murmured '*Buon giorno*' as Nicolò escorted her firmly across its vast expanse and up the staircase to their apartment.

'Nicolò...' she began a shade desperately as he pushed her gently across the threshold. 'I want to talk to you...'

'And I to you, Catia, but not on an empty stomach.'

Picking up a telephone, he tersely ordered breakfast to be sent to their apartment, before indicating that she should seat herself in one of the luxurious armchairs in the gracious sitting-room.

'So...' He regarded her steadfastly, looming over her as she obeyed his directive. 'Who was this man with whom you had an early morning assignation?'

'What did you say?' Astonishment brought the adrenalin flooding through her body, lending colour to her cheeks, forcing her pulse to a faster rhythm, just when she thought she had the situation under control. How dared he try to divert her accusations by making his own absurd allegations?

'You are neither deaf nor illiterate, *mia cara* Caterina,' he scolded softly. 'Neither are you stupid, although you appear not to grant me the same compliment. One moment you were with me last night—and the next one, gone. Do you think I didn't look for you? Or that I hadn't seen you in deep conversation with your male friend?'

'You saw me in the garden?' A nameless fear stirred inside her. 'But why didn't you join me?'

'You think I am so gauche that I would create a scene at my own promotion function?' A dark eyebrow lifted on the saturnine face. 'I didn't realise you had an acquaintance here in Venice. If the meeting had been innocent I would have expected you to introduce me to your companion. Last night I assumed that you were too tired for explanations and that in the morning when you awakened refreshed you would confide in me—and what do I find? An empty bed beside me. No note, nothing to suggest where I might find you. What else am I to expect, since you were not forcibly abducted, but that you had an assignation?'

Anger tightened Catia's diaphragm. How dared he attempt to turn the tables on her? Already he'd dropped the suave politeness he had worn in England, to show his true colours, revealing himself as an insolent stranger. Thank heavens she'd been prepared for the change.

'You arrogant——' she began, starting to rise to her feet, only to subside once more as after a discreet knock at the door a trolley was wheeled into the room by a young girl.

Aware of her heightened colour and the annoying trembling of her hands, Catia lowered her gaze to her own lap, clamping her lips together and mentally counting up to ten.

'Coffee?' Nicolò placed a cup on the low table at her side without waiting for her reply, as the maid withdrew. 'Croissants? Tomorrow you may choose your own breakfast, provided you don't intend to make any further early morning assignations. You were saying?' He raised his own cup to his lips as he awaited her reply.

There was only one way to fight fire—with fire. Inhaling a deep breath to steady her nerves, she lifted her small chin belligerently.

'That I would prefer you to treat me with the courtesy my position deserves!'

'Your position as my wife?' Dark eyes mocked her. 'But you are that in name only at the moment, my sweet. Depend upon it, whatever the position you assume in the next few minutes, I shall treat you with both courtesy and ardour.'

A pulse began to flutter in her throat as she read the unmistakable signs of desire mutating his strong face. With an effort she fought down a sense of rising panic.

'My position as the granddaughter of a *marchese*,' she corrected him evenly, her heart skipping a beat as she saw the betraying flicker of shock leap across his eyes, the slight tightening of his jaw which told her just what she wanted to know.

'So Antonio told you after all.' Danger explicit in every line of his fine body, he towered over her.

'Nonno? Good heavens, no.' Regardless of what he had done to her, she would protect her grandfather from Nicolò's wrath. 'I read some papers he'd received from Italy and left lying around on his desk,' she improvised quickly. 'I guess he's too old to bother about inheriting a title, but I'm not.' She paused to let her eyes move deliberately over the beautiful room. 'Particularly now I'm mistress of this *palazzo*! I've been planning all the fun I can have, all the entertaining I can do and parties I can give. For people of my own age, I mean, not the fuddy-duddies who were here last night...' Her voice tailed off into the brooding stillness of the room.

'I see,' Nicolò said at last. 'Well, *cara mia*, I hope you won't be too disappointed. You know as well as I that Italy is a republic. There is no recognised hierarchy of titles any more, and even if there were I doubt that the title of *marchesa* would pass to the present incumbent's granddaughter! These ex-titles had a tendency to pass to male heirs only. I imagine that was why your grandfather decided not to confide in you—because he recognises the incongruity of such a meaningless title.'

'Do you think so?' She aimed a smile at his stern face. 'I thought it might be because a title, of whatever origin, looks good on the letter heading of an ambitious charity...or company? Especially one exporting overseas to republics which have never had their own monarchy... And he didn't want to be troubled by unscrupulous companies trying to cash in on it.'

'I'm sure he had his reasons. They need not concern us, surely?' He regarded her with narrowed eyes and a hint of impatience in his manner.

'But he obviously told *you*.' She offered him a sweet smile, while her heart hammered frantically against her ribs. 'Or did you already know before you came to England on business?'

A stillness, terrifying in its impact, held his body immobile. 'What is this, Catia? The third degree? Do you charge me with some crime because I happened to be aware that your grandfather had inherited an impoverished and outdated title?'

'Of course not.' She took a final draught from her coffee-cup, before finding the strength to get to her feet with as much grace as was possible. So he was so sure of her that he wasn't even going to bother going through the motions of pleading innocence.

Once upright she felt emotionally stronger, although Nicolò still towered over her as she moved across to gaze out at the Grand Canal, now devoid of its veil of mist as the sun grew stronger. She would have felt less disadvantaged if she could have confronted him on the same level, but even her highest heels wouldn't have given her that equality!

'As a matter of fact I admire your single-mindedness in identifying an opportunity to improve your business image and pursuing it with such fervour.' She kept her eyes fixed on the leisurely progress of a gondola packed with Japanese tourists, who were benefiting from the stentorian tones of a gondolier accompanying himself on an accordion as he carolled a Venetian love-song, aware however that Nicolò's eyes were boring into the back of her head with something less than pleasure mirrored in their darkness if the tense atmosphere between them was anything to go on.

'Indeed, it seems that neither of us is a stranger to ambition if you saw marriage to me merely as a passport to an endless stream of socialising and parties, *cara mia*,' came the frighteningly soft reply.

'Oh, come now, Nicolò!' She turned to face him painting a facsimile of a smile on her soft mouth. 'A bargain's a bargain. Ours won't be the first marriage where a poor title marries wealth without breeding.' Alarmed by the flash of fury which sparkled in his eyes, she continued hurriedly, 'It's a much sounder basis for a relationship than delusions of love, don't you agree?'

She watched his expression harden as she waited with bated breath for his reply, one half of her praying against the odds that he would repeat his vows of love, the other coolly detached, expecting her worst fears to be confirmed.

As Nicolò's mouth twisted into a cruel smile she abandoned her last hope.

'So you were never fooled by my protestations of undying love, hmm?' He regarded her with narrowed eyes. 'I admit to being disappointed. I believed I had the art of courtship well mastered.'

'Oh, you have!' Catia assured him quickly. 'I was most impressed, but hardly taken in, especially as I suspected your motives from the start. It was a good game and we certainly played it well enough to fool my grandfather, but we're both old enough to know that love at first sight is a teenage syndrome rooted in fantasy and headed for disaster. The reality in our case was quite different. You saw having the granddaughter of a *marchese* as a business advantage and I wanted to escape from a dreary English village and a boring job to have some fun—buy clothes to fit my new status—have servants at my beck and call—live a little! But there's no need for us to keep up the pretence in private that we actually care for each other, is there?'

'Now that we no longer have to consider your grandfather's feelings, you mean?' came the gentle question from behind her. So gentle that it chilled her blood.

'I knew you'd understand!' She forced a smile to her wooden lips. 'It was in both our interests to deceive Nonno into believing I'd fallen in love with you, or he would never have agreed to our marrying. But I'm afraid I'm not a good enough actress to prolong the masquerade now we're alone. I assume that, as long as we keep up appearances in public, in private we can go our own ways.'

'Do you, now?' His measured tone was deceptively mild; only the brightness of his dark eyes betrayed that his apparent calmness was not genuine. 'Then I think I may safely say you assume too much, *mia dolce*.'

'Oh, surely not?' Catia protested, detesting the way he had called her his sweetness with such laboured sarcasm. 'I understand you already have a——' she paused delicately, drawing on her inner courage as his aggressively masculine proximity did nothing to dull her apprehension '—an ongoing liaison,' she finished abruptly.

Nicolò's eyes flamed at her, a formidable and powerful anger etched into every tense line of his aggressively held body.

'And who, I wonder, would be so unwise as to tell you that?' he asked softly.

'Someone . . . A man . . .' Despise him though she did, to offer Cesare Brunelli's name at that juncture was to expose him to a retribution she dared not think about. 'One of the guests at last night's party.'

'And was he so indiscreet as to mention the name of my *inamorata*?'

Catia stared up at him in mounting consternation, as his mouth thinned into a hard, angry line. But she'd already gone too far to retreat now, and, raw with the angry emotions which surged inside her, she wanted to see his reaction when he realised that his secret liaison wasn't so secret after all.

'Ah, your companion on the patio, no doubt.'

She didn't fail to catch the note of sarcasm in his voice.

'He said it was a matter of common speculation,' she offered with an indifferent shrug of her shoulders. 'Gina Cabrini, I think the name was. Was she at the party last night, Nicolò? I should have so liked to meet her. I understand you and she are such very good friends.'

'Then you understand correctly, *mia cara moglietta*.' A few steps and he was at her side, hands grasping her shoulders, pulling her body towards his own. 'I've known Gina since we were teenagers. She is married to one of my most trusted associates.'

'Separated from, you mean, surely?' She raised enquiring eyebrows. 'If my information is correct——'

'Enough of this gossip!'

The words died in her throat as Nicolò's head descended and his mouth imprisoned her lips, taking advantage of her gasp of surprise, to possess her mouth with shocking speed and purpose.

Automatically her hands rose to his shoulders to brace herself against his onslaught. For the first time since she had met him, he made no attempt to control or hide the arousal of his body as it hunted against hers.

Frustration—or was it anger?—lent his actions an intensity which shocked her as his tongue seduced her. A quiver of trepidation shuddered along her backbone as she read the strength of the desire which held him in its thrall, panic soaring through every cell of her body as in response to the fierce grasp of her fingers on his arm he finally relinquished the conquest of her mouth in order to trail his lips across the softness of her cheek.

'You have no need to be jealous of Gina!' Danger echoed in every husky syllable of the whisper as his sweet, warm breath assaulted her ear. 'If you had not been asleep when I came to bed I would have given you every proof you need that, whatever the motives behind our marriage, I intend it to be a real one in every sense of the word.'

'No...' It was a moan of protest, denying him the power to change the subject, to allay her fears with the undoubted skills of his powerful masculine body. She didn't want her anger aborted, crushed by the magic he could wield over her. But either he was far too aroused to hear her, or he chose to ignore her feeble protestation, as beneath her T-shirt his hand travelled her warm skin to cup one breast, only lightly shielded by a soft envelope of écru lace. For one wild moment she felt the desire to be naked in his arms, every inch of her vulnerable and offered for his caresses, as she experienced the hidden secret of his taut flesh responding under her own hands.

She was dissolving, her breasts aching, straining to fill his palms, as she fought the lethargy which threatened to overtake her mentally as well as physically. No! This wasn't what she wanted. This wasn't love; it was Nicolò's attempt to exert his authority over her, to punish her for seeing through his perfidy, to bind her with the undoubted charms of his body to the fate he had planned for her. It was a move she had to frustrate if she wished to keep even the dregs of her own integrity intact.

'*Basta*!' With a sharp cry she tore herself from his arms, stumbling towards the door, pulling it open, and running down the long corridor. With the advantage of surprise she might escape him, lose herself once more in the narrow streets of the city while she regrouped her senses and calmed herself enough to be able to face him again. A second time she would be armed against any physical approach he subjected her to!

Not pausing to glance over her shoulder, she made directly for the door which led into the street, knowing that at this time of day it would be unbolted. It was only when she had traversed several narrow streets at breakneck speed that she allowed herself to take a breather. Heart shuddering more from anxiety than effort, she leaned against a wall for a moment before peering round it carefully, back along the street from which she'd just come.

Nicolò had followed her! The streets were becoming well populated as early morning Venice swung into action to greet the day. Although several yards separated her from her avenging husband, Catia could see his dark head approaching at a speed which gave her no reason for optimism. He wasn't obviously hurrying, but the long, mean stride which was propelling him in her direction was eating up the distance between them.

There was no way he must catch up with her until she'd put her thoughts in order and formulated a plan of action! Fed by panic, she took to her heels, diving along alleyways, over bridges, mindless of direction, aware only that Nicolò was still on her trail, until to her horror she found herself in a dead end.

Before her lay one of the minor canals. A narrow walkway alongside it ended abruptly as the walls of adjacent buildings dipped directly into its still waters. Dear heavens! What could she do? Behind her the alleyway down which she had run stretched for several yards before she could hope to find another turn-off. The likelihood was that she would run directly into Nicolò's arms! And this area of the city was deserted! If his temper matched the animal-like stalk of his walk, then he could murder her and dispose of her body in the canal without anyone being the wiser—if he felt like it!

Then she saw it. Moored alongside a small flight of stone steps was a gondola, its interior carefully protected with a large red cover. If she could hide in there, Nicolò would think she had branched off before reaching the dead end! But with his knowledge of the city he would search here for her first! Without a second thought she scrambled into the gondola, managing to lift the cover without difficulty, pulling it across her shaking body, allowing only a tiny gap so that she could see if her fears would be realised.

They were. Only seconds after she had settled, her sharp ears detected the sound of approaching footsteps.

Now she knew the meaning of the phrase 'to have one's heart in one's mouth' as the footsteps came to a halt. From her hiding-place she could see the light grey casual shoes that Nicolò had been wearing, recognised the silver-grey of his elegantly cut trousers. She could even hear his steady breathing—or was it the echo of her own in that dusty, muffled place?

For what seemed a lifetime he stood there motionless, then he turned and walked away. She had fooled him! Or had she? She stayed where she was for another ten minutes before venturing out. Even then she half expected him to be lying in wait for her. But the surrounding alleyways were empty. Hardly believing her luck, she paused to consider her directions, then headed for the crowds she knew she would find around the Rialto Bridge.

She needed time to think, and she needed to have it without the fear of Nicolò prowling after her and pouncing on her. If only she could disguise her blonde hair, alter her clothes, mingle with the ever growing crowds of tourists...

It was the stalls in the streets of the Rialto which gave her the idea, and providence which abetted it. Thrusting her hand into the pocket of her jacket, she found half a dozen English five-pound notes, which she had secreted there instead of transporting them in her hand luggage. She had originally intended to change them into lire at a bank, but it was no secret that commercial centres would accept them at near face value.

It took but a few minutes to purchase a T-shirt with 'I love Venice' stencilled on it, and an imitation straw gondolier's hat sporting a red ribbon. Since she would need somewhere to change she entered a small boutique and, having bought a pair of scarlet shorts, took the opportunity of changing into the whole ensemble in the shop.

Nicolò would never recognise her now! With her hair twisted up beneath the hat and her long legs exposed beneath the short shorts, the garish T-shirt straining across her full breasts, she looked the epitome of a typical tourist, the type of woman that Nicolò would dismiss disdainfully as improperly dressed for the dignity of Venice! But the streets of the Rialto were narrow. Her disguise would be even more foolproof in the spacious Piazza of San Marco.

Following the clearly posted tourist signs, she arrived some fifteen minutes later at her destination. If San Marco's had appeared imposing from the Grand Canal, then seen from her emergence at the far end of the Piazza it was spectacular, its great arches, domes and pinnacles glistening white and gold in the heady Italian sunlight, the great column of its separate campanile pointing a green-tipped finger into the blue vault of heaven.

In that instant Catia's problems took second place to the feeling of joy and happiness which thrilled through her. This was her father's country, part of her own heritage, and nothing should mar her exultation in it! Approaching the Basilica by way of one of the arcades around the perimeter of the Piazza, its diamond-patterned stones clean and litter-free beneath her soft-soled feet, she gazed in awe at the expensive jewellery and handworked-linen shops which lined it, before leaving its shade to walk across the centre of the square.

Here groups of tourists fed flocks of pigeons while souvenir stands abounded. Dodging the crowds, she approached the Basilica itself, to stand staring at its ornate façade. Before she realised what was about to happen she found herself engulfed by a crowd of people, obviously tourists who must have entered the Piazza from the direction of the Grand Canal.

Behind her a woman's voice raised to a lecturer's resonance began to address the small flock in excellent English.

'The Church of San Marco, or the Golden Basilica, as it is also known, is another of the splendid examples of why Venice bears not only the title of La Serenissima, the serene one, but also that of the Mistress of Gold. It was initiated in the High Middle Ages when——'

'Hey, I haven't seen you on the ship before!' A male voice broke into Catia's concentration, and she half turned to find herself being addressed by a personable young man about her own age.

'No, well...' she hedged, beginning to see the advantage of being a member of a crowd. 'I mean, it's a big ship, isn't it?' A reasonable statement in view of size being relative, and the number of people clustered around the guide.

'Yeah, sure.' He cast her a speculative look. 'I don't know about you, but I've had enough of this culture business to last me a lifetime. I can get all these facts from a guidebook if I want to, but I'm dying for a long, cold beer. What say we slope off and try to find a bar or café somewhere?'

'OK.' Catia nodded her approval. A swift glance around the Piazza showed no obvious sign of Nicolò, but it wouldn't hurt to become part of a twosome, if only as a temporary measure, and after all the tension she had experienced her own mouth and throat were parched.

'This way, then.' Slipping his arm round her waist in friendly camaraderie, he led her towards the Grand Canal. 'I spotted a whole row of bars along the waterfront. We can sit down, have a drink, watch the world go by, and exchange notes about each other.'

'Why not?' Catia allowed herself to be ushered briskly towards their destination, only too pleased to sit down in a comfortable basket-weave chair under a deep red sunshade while her companion ordered his own beer and a Coke for her.

The view was dazzling: *vaporetti*, the urban waterbuses of Venice, leaving their stops for the other islands in the Lagoon and the famous Lido, gondolas bobbing up and down at one of their numerous stations, water taxis plying their trade, and, across the vast open pavement which separated the bar from the canal itself, a never-ending parade of people, walking, admiring, and buying souvenirs from the plethora of stalls. Here she could relax, certain that even if Nicolò was still pursuing her he would never find her.

'I think perhaps, *cara mia*, that you have enjoyed a free rein for long enough and the time has come for me to escort you back to the *palazzo*, no?' There was no mistaking that voice or the menace behind the gently couched question.

'Nicolò!' He had crept up on her from behind, insinuating his lean frame between the tables to stand with a proprietorial hand on her shoulder.

'Now, wait a moment...' Catia's companion sprang to his feet. 'This lady's with me. We're on the same cruise. Why don't you go away and try your luck elsewhere?'

'And your name is?' The dulcet tones were ominous, as Catia tried vainly to get her companion's attention, to prevent him from making further claims he couldn't substantiate.

'Sherman—Gordon Sherman, if it's anything to do with you.' Not lacking courage, he took a deep draught of lager before rising to his feet. 'And I advise you——'

'No! *I* advise *you* to stay silent.' There was no mistaking the venom underlying Nicolò's cold tones. 'Your so-called cruise companion just happens to be my wife, and you just happen to have interrupted our honeymoon!'

'Nicolò, please...' Sick with apprehension, Catia, too, stumbled to her feet. 'Mr Sherman made a natural mistake and I didn't enlighten him.' Her eyes beseeched his stern face, hoping to discover some tiny sign of mercy, but failing miserably. 'I was thirsty, and when he offered to buy me a Coke...' She gestured down to her still full glass.

'You must allow me to reimburse you. How much, Signor Sherman?' Nicolò raised disdainful eyebrows at the young Englishman, who was gawping at him with all the lifelessness of a fish on a slab.

'I had no idea...I thought... She didn't say anything...'

'Well, silence is golden, they say.' Nicolò shrugged indolent shoulders, before dipping a hand into his pocket. 'Here, take this; it should cover your costs and inconvenience.'

'Yes, right... I'm sorry about the misunderstanding...' The other man accepted the money without looking at it, and drained his glass before casting Catia a pained look and leaving the bar with his shoulders hunched and his hands in the pockets of his jeans.

Oh, dear heavens! What was going to happen now? The brooding expression on Nicolò's face promised her little mercy. Did he intend to drag her back to the *palazzo* through the streets of Venice? She bit her lip in anguish. And, if so, what would he do to her when he had her in its lonely confines?

CHAPTER FIVE

'MARCHESA, please be seated.' With exemplary courtesy Nicolò arranged her chair so that she could sink once more on to it. 'You look as if you need to finish your drink.'

The sardonic use of the title he had dismissed so contemptuously brought a flush of colour to Catia's cheeks, but she obeyed his instruction. Not only because she needed a cool drink, but also because the longer she could remain in a public place the better she considered her eventual chances of conducting a civilised conversation with him to be.

'*Un caffè nero, per favore*.' An autocratic hand dismissed a hovering waiter for his pleasure, before Nicolò seated himself opposite her, leaning back in his chair, long legs splayed out beneath the table, narrowed eyes regarding her enigmatically. 'Well, that was quite a chase you led me, *angelo mio*.'

'How did you find me?' Catia asked reluctantly.

'Find you?' Nicolò's short bark of laughter was both self-satisfied and triumphant. 'I never lost you. But an astute hunter never follows his prey into a burrow. Besides, I had no wish to take an early morning dip in one of Venice's less salubrious canals, and that surely would have been the outcome for both of us if I'd attempted to prise you out of your hiding-place in that gondola.'

Mortified, Catia stared at his complacent expression. Ten minutes she'd spent in that suffocating prison and all the time he'd known she was there! He must have found some vantage-point she'd overlooked and waited until she had emerged, before following her again.

'I'm surprised you didn't pounce on me before now,' she told him stiffly.

'And spoil an amusing chase?' He smiled, but although his beautiful mouth curved appreciatively his dark eyes remained still and watchful, devoid of humour. 'Although I must admit that when you emerged from that boutique dressed like a cartoon figure of an undesirable tourist I needed to exercise a great deal of restraint to stop myself from grabbing hold of you then and there, and removing you from public view!' A scathing glance reinforced his disgust. 'I can hardly remove your appalling clothing now without causing a riot, and revealing to the public that which I prefer to reserve for my personal perusal, but I'd appreciate your doing me the courtesy of taking off that absurd hat.'

All that effort, all that heartache and he had been watching her all the time, toying with her like an angler with a fish, knowing that whenever he liked he could reel her in!

'You were enjoying yourself!' she accused coldly, deciding to humour him by obeying his request, abandoning the gondolier's boater and allowing her hair to fall in wild confusion round her face.

He nodded. 'Until you decided to find yourself a boyfriend. Then I knew the time had come to intervene.' There was a dangerous glint in his eyes as he observed her over the rim of his coffee-cup. 'I admit this is not the way I envisaged the start of our married life together, but it is not entirely without its merits. The blood of the hunter always races faster after the chase—and capture.'

They were not the words Catia wanted to hear. Neither was the expression on Nicolò's lean, handsome face reassuring. A shudder of apprehension trembled through her. Reluctantly she admitted that despite what she had already learned she had not managed to conquer her own wilful desire for him. She could fight this traitorous weakness while she was allowed to keep her distance, but how could she ever fight his seduction when her whole body still craved the solace of his? Her only hope must lie in masking her vulnerability by verbal attack.

'I'm surprised you know anything about hunting. I thought you came from a long line of peasant farmers,' she retorted with a lift of her eyebrows.

'Ah hah! I suppose I owe your companion of last night thanks for that observation, as well. Suddenly I'm not good enough for the *marchese's* granddaughter after all—is that it, Catia?' A low note of bitterness echoed in the question. 'You were prepared to humble yourself to wed a mere commoner when you discovered he was wealthy, but now you find he has the background of a peasant you wish to withdraw from the bargain?' He gave a short bark of humourless laughter. 'Well, I'm afraid you've discovered that fact too late. But if you're thinking of exercising the natural superiority which the old aristocracy claimed, I'd like to remind you that it's no longer considered the right of a wealthy landowner to set his dogs on a poor peasant whose only crime was to cross his boundary in search of a few fallen pieces of fruit.'

'Dogs?' One look at the brooding passion of his face and she knew Nicolò was speaking literally. Her feeling of foreboding deepened. 'Someone set dogs on you?'

He uttered a harsh laugh. 'Not me—my father. He was fourteen at the time, and if it hadn't been for the intervention of a friend he would have had his throat torn out.'

'But that's appalling!' Catia's natural sympathy broke through the patina of nonchalance she had adopted.

'Yes, isn't it? But don't let it bother you too much, Marchesa. None of us is able to choose his ancestors.'

It was a couple of seconds before the import of what he was imputing dawned on her.

'You mean it was one of my ancestors who set the dogs on your father?' she asked, horrified.

'Leopoldo Guido Lorenzo, Marchese di Castellone.' Nicolò pushed his chair back, regained his feet and placed a handful of *lire* on the table without counting them. 'Shall we go, Catia? Back to my *palazzo* to redress old wrongs?'

'For pity's sake, Nicolò...' Despair clouded Catia's light blue eyes as she tried to read the expression on his lean, handsome face. Sombre and unsmiling, his eyes told her nothing. Was this the final entry on the ledger? The third and perhaps most compelling reason that Nicolò had hunted her down in England, after learning of her existence? Her mouth dry, she made a vain attempt to moisten her lips. It made a terrible kind of sense, although the justice was perverted. By making her his wife, did Nicolò intend to subjugate her in the same way that the old *marchese* had abused his sovereignty over the people who lived and worked on his land? No—she brushed a lock of hair from her forehead—surely that was rubbish? The stuff of nightmares? Yet it would explain so much. Three reasons, each one alone insufficient to warrant Nicolò's journey from Italy—but together...

'Are you telling me that there is a feud between our families?' she enquired boldly.

'Not any more, *amore mio*.' His soft reply did nothing to quieten the rapid beat of her heart, as his mouth curved into a slow smile. 'Relax, Catia. There are no dogs in the *palazzo*. Your lovely neck is safe in my keeping.' His warm brown palm reached out to caress her throat with the delicacy of a butterfly's wing. 'We have made a bargain, you and I, and, whatever our motives, there are other much more enjoyable ways of healing the hatred of the past. Come, my patience is becoming sorely strained by your reluctance to honour your commitment!'

She took his peremptorily extended hand because she had no other option. She couldn't run from him forever. Despite the fact that he'd left her in no doubt of his immediate intentions she was hopeful that, after they'd trudged through the hot streets of the city, most of his desire for retribution would have evaporated. Enough, at least, for her to be able to dissuade him by a display of apathy.

'Nicolò!' Forced abruptly from her reverie, she screeched his name in protest as her hand was grasped and she found herself hoisted into his arms, his other arm firmly beneath her knees. 'What are you doing?'

'Taking you home—what else?' He strode out into the sunshine, the mass of pedestrians between themselves and the Grand Canal parting to let him through. 'You didn't think I was going to walk through the streets of Venice accompanied by a scarecrow, did you? As soon as I saw you settled down at the bar I phoned the *palazzo* and told Giovanni to bring the launch to meet us.'

Smiling smugly, he carried her down to a small pontoon and handed her over to the waiting boatman. Embarrassed by the knowing looks which followed their progress, Catia gritted her teeth and remained silent.

Well might Nicolò wear the triumphant smile of victory, she thought sourly, as the sleek launch moved slowly away towards its destination. What she had seen as a generous gesture on his part—his allowing her to stay and finish her drink—had been nothing more than a respite to enable him to summon transport. At least she could be grateful for the speed limit on the Canal, imposed to prevent the wash from high-speed vessels wearing away the foundations of the old buildings. It gave her a few more minutes to consider her next plan of action.

Even then, the journey took a far shorter time than she had hoped for.

'Should I lock and bolt the doors or have you tired of your game of hide-and-seek?' Nicolò purred as he escorted her through the entrance door to their apartment.

'It's no game,' she returned sharply. 'We both had our reasons for marrying each other, and since love never entered into the equation it seems pretty pointless to pretend that it did.'

'Who mentioned love?' He surveyed her dispassionately. 'You have the face of an angel, Catia, and the body of a Jezebel. Attributes to arouse the Casanova in any red-blooded man, and, as you've already discovered, *carissima*, my blood is more red than blue. We made a tacit bargain, did we not? An arrangement to further our separate ambitions? I to supply you with material benefits as befit your mercenary little heart in exchange for the advantages your presence in my household will bring.' He paused deliberately before adding, 'And one of those advantages will be to enjoy the comfort of your nubile body when the mood takes me.'

'And risk enraging Gina?' Catia retorted, flinching from his cold-blooded analysis of their relationship.

'Gina has no say in anything I choose to do!' His eyes sparkled with a chilling arrogance. 'And it will be in your best interests not to suggest that she has, or you will live to regret it. As for this show of reluctance on your part to seal our bargain, I would advise you to remember that your grandfather is an old man, and would react badly to any suggestion that you married me for any other reason than that you loved me. I'm sure, whatever other failings you have, you wouldn't wish to cause him further anguish.'

Catia sucked her breath in, unable to suppress the twinge of anxiety she felt at what was obviously a veiled threat. Further anguish? What previous anguish had her beloved Nonno been caused at the hand of this impertinent peasant?

Hiding her pain, she shrugged, desperately afraid that she was fighting a losing battle but determined to fight to the bitter end. 'If you want variety in sex I'm sure there are plenty of other women who will provide it for you—and willingly.' Deliberately she turned her back on him dismissively.

'Of course.' His deep voice was matter-of-fact. 'But I grow tired of eager, willing women. Do you know,

Catia, I have never in my life bedded a virgin, and the mood is on me to put that situation right.'

'What?' She spun round, her chest tightening in fear, her voice faltering as she read the adamantine purpose on his hard face.

'And you are a virgin, aren't you, Catia?' he continued inexorably. 'Your grandfather assured me that you were, and in the circumstances I don't think he would have lied to me.'

'He had no right to assure you of anything of the kind!' she protested fiercely, as she felt the net closing round her. There was no way this autocratic man she had once mistakenly thought she loved beyond reason was going to allow her to retain her independence. He wanted everything from her. Not content with flaunting her as his wife in public in order to enhance his image and hide his infidelities, he intended to humiliate her in private as payment for the sins of her ancestors, and there was nothing she could do about it!

'Perhaps not,' Nicolò's voice intruded through the haze of pain which engulfed her, 'but he wanted to ensure that I didn't hurt you through ignorance of your innocence...and neither shall I, if that is what is making you behave like a frightened faun.' His pause was minimal. 'Or are you telling me your grandfather was labouring under a misapprehension?'

'Would it make any difference?' she asked through clenched teeth.

'No.' He shook his dark head. 'Be assured that I'm a practised and considerate lover regardless of my partner's experience. Depend on it, I will hide my disappointment if I find out that you have been lying, although I cannot promise not to demand a forfeit from you for your deception. Shall we dispense with this abomination?'

Not waiting for her reply as she cringed away from him, he took the hem of her T-shirt, lifting the garment and pulling it over her head to discard it disdainfully on the floor.

Catia's face flushed, partly from embarrassment, partly because of his lackadaisical admission of sexual expertise and partly from a rising tide of awareness which appeared to be turning her body to aspic, and replacing her initial terror. How dared he boast of his conquests with such unmitigated arrogance? Running her fingers through her tousled hair, she whispered with a note of desperation, 'This isn't what I want...'

'So you insist.' He eyed her mutinous expression as if to evaluate its sincerity. 'Then what do you want? That I should seek out the man whom you met on the terrace last night and again this morning and challenge him to a duel to prove that I don't intend to stand for any more nonsense from you? Believe me, I would do it with pleasure, but duelling is not among my many talents and I might lose. Or would you prefer to be my widow rather than my wife, hmm?'

'Don't joke like that, Nicolò!' For a few seconds all the discarded emotions she had harboured for him rose in a gush as her horrified eyes remonstrated with him. Afraid he would read her feelings too clearly, she rushed on, 'Besides, I've told you already that I had no assignation this morning. The man on the terrace last night was a stranger to me. He introduced himself as a journalist—Cesare Brunelli—and said he had been invited.'

'Brunelli—ah, yes.' Nicolò pursed his strong mouth. 'The name is familiar to me. Not a man to trust, *moglie mia*.'

'Is any man?' Catia asked bitterly, flinching from the unwanted title of 'wife'.

'As much as any woman, I dare say,' Nicolò countered. 'And probably more than most.' His hand reached out towards her, taking her arm with purposeful fingers. 'This is not quite the atmosphere I envisaged in which to introduce you to your new duties,' he murmured. 'But it will suffice.'

Despair weakened her resolve. Suddenly Catia knew she couldn't fight him on this front any longer. Already she'd persuaded him that she was venal and self-interested, and in so doing had removed herself from any sense of chivalry which might have lurked behind his cruel façade.

At the time it had seemed the only recourse to salve her battered pride, but she'd been a fool to dream that she might be able to repulse him long enough for him to lose interest in her. Wearily she conceded that to prolong the fight to keep her physical independence would make his eventual triumph over her all the sweeter.

Sensing her mental surrender, Nicolò's arm encompassed her trembling form, gathering her quiescent body towards his own eager flesh. Warm and trembling, Catia's skin shimmered with an electric response at his practised touch and she found herself returning the ardent pressure of his mouth which sought and imprisoned her own. There was only one way she could survive this ordeal—by pretending that Nicolò truly loved her; forcing her mind back to the past; recalling that morning when she'd come back from her ride and seen him waiting for her.

It was easier, far easier than she had imagined. Aching for the illusion of love which had been so cruelly snatched away from her, she sighed her satisfaction as Nicolò's fingers lifted the heavy fall of blonde hair from her neck, his eager fingers caressing the delicate nape, spreading to tease the soft pink lobes of her ears, as her mind blocked out the disillusionment and horror of the previous twelve hours.

She heard the increased power of his breathing, felt the heavy hammer of his heart as it echoed against her barely covered breasts, and the illusion was complete. Responding with a blind passion, she exchanged caress for caress, returning his eager kisses with an ardour of her own, feeling her body mutate still further as nature fashioned it to receive and enjoy her lover.

Her lover—that was it! A man to pleasure her. A man she need harbour no love or loyalty towards. A man whom she would force to discard her as soon as she felt it safe to do so without imperilling her grandfather. Only that way would she be able to play the part Nicolò demanded and keep her self-respect. If he had thought to subjugate her by possessing her, she would show him that he had failed.

He was still kissing her when he swung her up into his arms and carried her through to the bedroom, bearing her down against the softness of the bed by the weight of his own ardent body.

With urgent hands he discarded her bra, swearing softly under his breath when his fingers trembled clumsily at the fastening to her shorts. Uttering a tiny murmur, she pushed his palm away, divesting herself of her flimsy garments with a natural grace.

'Wait.' He curled off the bed to regain his feet, his eyes gleaming and mesmeric beneath hooded lids, commanding her full attention as with a slow, easy, masculine paucity of movement he stripped his fine body naked, every controlled action an arrogant statement of his physical perfection. 'Now, Catia *mia*, I shall teach you exactly what I require from the woman who bears my name.'

He was breathing deeply, harshly as he leant over her to bury his head in the pale orbs of her breasts, his mouth seeking the darker beauty of their apices, worshipping them with a gentle but persistent salutation which had her reaching her hands to his hair, running them down his neck, touching the hard bones of his cheek and jaws as he pleasured her beyond all belief.

'Oh, Nicolò! *Mio caro amore*...' The words of love sprang to her lips and were bitten back at the last moment as she entered unknown territory, depending on the man who had tricked her with such expertise to be her guide, the husky brokenness of her voice telling him of her fear mingled with delight. Gently he eased her away from him so that he could spread his hard masculine frame beside her on the bed, throwing an imprisoning leg across her thighs, so that their bodies came into shocking, intimate contact.

Eyes closed as his seeking mouth captured and nibbled at her lower lip, Catia felt the throbbing pulse of her own body respond to Nicolò's powerful arousal.

'*Marchesa mia*...' he purred against her cheek, then her mouth, trailing his lips down her arching throat, kissing the delicate curve of her breastbone, while his hands, tanned against the soft golden gleam of her unexposed skin, traced the curves and undulations of her willing body with a gentleness that was tormenting.

Gone now were any emotional inhibitions Catia might have felt, as her physical needs superimposed themselves. Only for a brief space of time did she wonder bitterly how any man could be so tender, so controlled and yet so alive with trembling desire when he was extorting vengeance for old wrongs.

'Caterina...' He expelled her name on a sigh as she stirred against him, her hands reaching for the satin skin of his naked back. With disciplined fingers she explored the long stretch of his spine, traced the outline of his ribs, enjoyed the sensation of his shoulderblades as they moved smoothly beneath their covering of heated flesh.

She had been trained to understand the composition of the human body, taught the relationship between bone and muscle: at any other time could have put a name to each joint and sinew that stirred beneath her touch. But now, all she was conscious of was that every part belonged to the whole composite magic which was Nicolò. Unwanted or not, he was her husband, and by enjoying him she would deplete his pride of conquest!

Nothing mattered now except their mutual need, the satisfaction of this wild, building torment which was forcing small whimpers of demand from her half-closed mouth. When Nicolò's hand crept downwards from her waist, his caressing fingers trailing their sorcery, Catia gasped, and, when they discovered that she was ready and aching for the culmination of their lovemaking, shock reverberated through her, her body jerking almost uncontrollably as it was racked with a hunger she had never imagined possible.

Nicolò muttered something incomprehensible beneath his breath as he reached towards his own body, but Catia was quicker; seizing the initiative, she guided him to her, offering herself for his conquest, crying out her joy as he made her body his own without pain or difficulty, filling her with his heat and warmth and power. Filling and completing her, making her one with him.

In a movement of innate knowledge she bent her legs, rocking back on her hips, inviting, alluring, demanding... and Nicolò did not disappoint her, as her hand fanned over his broad back and she felt the heady tumult of his heart and the betraying dampness of his fine skin.

With a master's touch he loved and incited her, drawing her steadily along the road to fulfilment until she gasped out his name, quickening the syllables in tune with her own rhythm until the final, soaring moment of release. She was still making incomprehensible ecstatic mews of pleasure when Nicolò achieved his own summit within her velvet fastness. His full weight pressed her contented body into the mattress for only a few seconds before he gained enough control to roll away from her, to lie on his back, one arm thrown across his closed eyes as his breath sawed in his chest.

Bit by bit Catia's body returned from the floating limbo which had overtaken it. Her heart regained its steady rhythm; her mind cleared although a pleasant lethargy held her spread in wanton abandonment on the soft cover. Gradually the euphoria that had unleashed her unquestioning responses began to fade, to be replaced by a sense of shame.

Nicolò's performance as a lover had been magnificent. Caring, passionate and sensitive. But it had been only that—a performance—she reminded herself. Carried out by a consummate actor who had already trod many other stages.

She stole a sidelong look at Nicolò's profile as it lay on the pillow beside her, enjoying the physical beauty of his strong face—the broad forehead and sculptured brows, the deep-set eyes with their thick splayed lashes, the dominant nose with its straight, proud bone and flaring nostrils, the sensitive, passionate mouth, full and firm, carved by a master hand—and felt desolation enter her soul.

He had initiated her into the joys of love, reading the message her body had given him, waiting until she'd become totally relaxed and unafraid so that he could take her painlessly through barriers that existed more in the mind than in the delicate construction of a woman's anatomy. If only there had been no other motive in his actions other than their mutual satisfaction. How could she ever ease the torment of her mind when even the anaesthesia of passion was so short-lasting?

'Well, Marchesa, did your peasant lover please you?'

For the first time she saw the light of his dark pupils behind the lowered lashes and realised that he had been returning her stare.

A shiver of foreboding touched her naked skin, and she hunched her body into a sitting position, hugging her knees to her chest, hiding the opaline gleam of her breast from his marauding gaze in a quaint gesture of modesty.

'Don't call me that, please, Nicolò,' she exhorted quietly.

'I thought you liked it, *cara*?' he purred. 'Isn't it your passport to fame and fortune?'

Catia stirred uncomfortably, as she was forced to face reality. 'You belittle it when you use it with such sarcasm,' she retorted stiffly.

'Ah hah! You grant a lowly peasant the use of your body, but begrudge him the use of your title, *signora*?' he suggested, his face unreadable, his voice tinged with an emotion which was neither laughter nor anger, but an odd amalgam of both.

'Don't be absurd, Nicolò!' she rebuked him, asperity sharpening her tone. 'I can't imagine anyone less worthy of the title "lowly", either in terms of birth, achievement or personality, than you, regardless of what your ancestors did for a living!'

'A pity,' he mused provocatively, lethargically arranging his vibrant body into a sitting position so that he could reach towards her and wind his fingers through her mane of golden hair. 'Because the world is full of stories about beautiful titled women lusting after the lower classes. Catherine the Great was reputed to have ordered the lowest ranks of her soldiers to attend her bedchamber, provided they had the attributes of beauty and strength necessary to pleasure her...' With slow determination he drew her head backwards, leaning over her to take her mouth in a deep, searchingly passionate act of possession.

Blindingly aware of the perfume of his skin, the clean masculine taste of him and the restrained power which lay dormant beneath his satin flesh, Catia could only endure the tender violation to which he subjected her. She knew instinctively that to return it would have been to reignite the fires which lay slumbrous just below the surface of his being, and something deep inside her warned her against such a course.

'*Mia bella Caterina*...' The husky whisper left the passage of its breath on her cheek, as he lifted his mouth but a few inches clear of her face, and he raised his other hand to trace her profile with a gentle finger. 'Then there was Lady Chatterley, who found solace in the arms of her gamekeeper. Is that what you would like—to turn the hunter into a gamekeeper?' he enquired smoothly.

Painfully aware that nothing about her remained a secret to the man who had shared his name and his body with her, she took refuge in evasion, saying lightly, 'You've got your proverbs mixed. It's the poacher who turns into the gamekeeper, not the hunter, but I admit that you are a competent lover, although I have no means of comparison.'

'Nor shall you have!' He turned, his movements fluid as a cat's. 'Your place is with me and me only!'

'You make it sound as if I'm your prisoner instead of your wife,' Catia protested, forcing a note of indignation into her voice, as she recalled the part she had opted to play.

He flexed his shoulder muscles. 'Your surroundings and your diet are considerably better than any prisoner would enjoy, and I am more demanding than a gaoler would dare to be. Ours may not be a love match, but that is all to the good, since we start life together with no false expectations. It is an added advantage that we are physically compatible, and as long as you heed my instructions I'm sure we will both get out of this union exactly what we want. Provided you don't cross me, you'll find I can be a considerate husband. As proof of which, I've ordered a splendid lunch to be served to us on the terrace in an hour's time, and afterwards you shall choose how you wish to spend the rest of the day. Can I be more fair than that?'

'No,' Catia agreed quietly. She had no wish to fight him overtly at that moment, not now, when her whole being was relaxed and lethargic from their lovemaking. He had won the first battle, and for the time being she was content to allow him his sense of victory; but there would be many more battles before this war was over, she thought wearily. In the meantime she must bide her time until she discovered the nature of the hold Nicolò had over Nonno, and determine how she could break it once and for all without endangering the old man's future. Only then would she be free to escape from the bondage which enthralled her.

CHAPTER SIX

THEY lunched on *risotto primavera*, a rice dish served with minced fresh vegetables, followed by Adriatic sole in a sweet and sour sauce served with white asparagus and wild mushrooms and then a creamy trifle of custard and liqueur sponge cake, with a light Italian vanilla ice-cream to round the meal off and cleanse the palate. Nicolò had requested mineral water and a bottle of Soave to accompany the meal, both bottles reaching the table in an ice-bucket, their sides misted and dewed, their coolness a refreshing contrast to the delicious food.

Refusing the offer of a liqueur to accompany the rich dark coffee which completed the meal, Catia watched Nicolò indulging himself with an Amaretto, taking it with him to the long, swinging canopied seat which over-looked the Grand Canal.

Her coffee finished, she joined him, subsiding on the soft cushions, her whole body glowing with a sense of well-being, her emotional pain temporarily allayed by the wild happiness of sharing the peace and beauty of the garden and its outlook with the man who, despite everything she had learned about him, could still make her beleaguered heart beat faster.

'Here...' He offered his brandy glass to her with a careless insolence. 'Warm it between your breasts for me and turn a fine liqueur into a drink for the gods.'

Wordlessly, she obeyed him, nestling the cool balloon glass against the bare skin of her cleavage visible above the neckline of the soft pink silk dress she'd chosen to wear after her shower, handing it back to him when the glass no longer felt cold.

Cupping it in his palms, Nicolò lifted it to his face, savouring the aroma, before sipping the contents with the air of a connoisseur.

'Perfect.' He allowed his eyes to drift over her reclining body. 'The scent of almonds mixed with the scent of my lover.' He ran his tongue over his full firm lips. 'The taste of passion and desire. Tomorrow we must go to the priest and arrange for the church to recognise our union, *amore mio*. I think perhaps the church of Santa Maria dei Miracoli, otherwise known as the *scrigno d'oro*, would be the perfect setting for you.'

'The golden jewel box?' Catia translated, inwardly wincing at the casual endearment, her heart pitching disturbingly at this new assault on her breached defences. 'It sounds beautiful.'

'The most beautiful church in the world,' Nicolò agreed. 'Small but exquisite, and the perfect ambience for the golden jewel I myself possess.' He lifted his free hand and stroked the soft fall of Catia's beautiful hair as it caressed her shoulders, but there was no affection in his glance to soften the hard glitter of his dark eyes. 'Tomorrow too we shall discuss the guest list and arrange for the invitations to be sent, but the mood is on me to be generous so for the rest of today we will do what pleases you.'

Now was the time to tell him she had no intention of hallowing their civil union in church, but the words to oppose him refused to come to her tongue. Mellowed by his passionate possession, her hormones refused to surge to her rescue and endow her with the anger she needed to challenge his plan of action. Besides, once she had made her point the situation between them was sure to deteriorate, and some part of her psyche ached to prolong this period of truce between them.

'Could we just stay here and talk for a while?' she asked hesitantly, drowsy from the effect of the fine wine and the scent of privet, her senses calmed by the warmth of the day, the showy beauty of the scarlet hibiscus in full bloom now in the nearby flowerbed and the lazy activity taking place on the Grand Canal.

'What would you like to talk about?' Nicolò's lips were soft and warm against her face, his breath sweet with the scent of *Amaretto* as he brushed them along the line of her cheekbone, the action a statement of the proprietorship he had established so recently over her weaker body.

'Your future plans,' she told him. 'For instance, how long will we stay in Venice?'

'Until the church blesses our union.' His predatory fingers caressed the soft curve of her breast, causing her to strain away from him, uneasily aware that her flesh lacked the discretion of her emotions. 'I intend that my *marchesa* shall have a wedding which reflects her nobility. She shall be transported to the church in a gondola strewn with roses, and wearing a dress which befits her beauty.'

'Are you serious?' Doubly glad that she had no intention of complying with his plans, she felt obliged to challenge his response. Even if she had still been labouring under the illusion that he loved her, she would have balked at his making her the centre of attention for the many tourists in the city.

'Of course. What else? In a city where there are no roads everything goes by water...funerals, weddings. Also you shall have an escort of gondoliers serenading you with a traditional Venetian *bacarolle*. It is no more than my family will expect from me. They have waited a long time to see me take a wife, and although my father appreciates the reason for your grandfather's insistence on a civil ceremony before you left England he will not be content until he sees us properly married, and in a style which is a credit to the status of our family.'

'What—no Neapolitan love-song to add to the aura of romance?' Catia raised her eyebrows sardonically, deciding not to comment on his scathing opinion of the ceremony carried out at Suddingham. In her opinion it had been only too proper—a contract not as easily broken as she would have wished!

'A tourist preference, and not to my liking.' He shrugged broad shoulders. 'Venice has a rich heritage of its own, one we should respect.'

So it was his intention to parade her before the populace like the prize won by a conquering hero, was it? To impress whom? The husband of Gina Cabrini, probably, she accorded bitterly, as much as his family.

'And afterwards?' Her mouth strangely dry, she raised her clear eyes to survey the carved planes of his prepossessing face.

'We will enjoy our wedding-night as we should have enjoyed last night. And as we have enjoyed this morning. What else?' He lofted his dark eyebrows in her direction.

'I meant how soon will we leave Venice after the ceremony?' Quickly she corrected herself, rejecting his unwanted promise of further humiliating seduction.

'As soon as possible.' He stretched his long legs, lifting his face towards the summer sky. 'I admit I shall regret saying *addio* to Venezia, but already there is work piling up in Milan which needs my attention. So it's a case of making the most of our honeymoon before our wedding. At least we have your grandfather to thank for ensuring that our union is recognised by the state, so we shall not become the victims of the scandalmongers while we are waiting for the essential plans to be put in hand.'

Catia glanced away from Nicolò's lounging figure, cloaking the pain in her eyes as she thought of her grandfather. Oh, Nonno, she wailed silently, how could you give your blessing to such a *mésalliance*? How could you condemn me to a loveless marriage? Perhaps she should hate her grandfather, but all she felt for the old man was compassion, knowing that he must have been placed under considerable duress to betray her in such a manner.

'I shall have to send him and Aunt Becky a postcard tomorrow,' she remarked coolly, then, dragging her mind back to the present, determined not to reveal her true reactions, 'Tell me again about your apartment in Milan.'

In the swift, sweet days of their psuedo-courtship in Suddingham, Nicolò had spoken about the large apartment in Milan where he spent most of his time. Now at her instigation he told her again, describing the location and the furnishings, telling her about the city and its parks, giving her a detailed and colourful picture of the shops and entertainment centres which awaited her, from the local cinema to the glory of La Scala.

As the sun gradually became lower in the sky and the air lost its primary warmth, she tried to maintain an atmosphere of normality, knowing that, whatever problems the future held, this one day of fantasy would live forever in her memory. So she listened politely while he reiterated the pleasures which awaited her in Milan.

Under her gentle prompting he told her about his friends and colleagues, and more about the nature of his work; of his hopes and ambitions to design cars which were not only beautiful and efficient but incorporated the highest safety factors. He spoke with a glowing enthusiasm about his plans so that she found herself caught up in his vibrant excitement, encouraging him to expound his theories, questioning him about the technicalities with a burgeoning interest which took even her by surprise, since she had no intention of sharing his life for any longer than was necessary.

It was dusk when he rose leisurely to his feet and held out his hand to assist her to do likewise. 'Any more questions, Catia?' he asked lazily. 'I had no idea you were so interested in what I do for a living.'

For those few precious moments she realised their rapport had been so intense that she'd fooled herself into believing they truly cared for each other. Concerned that her eager response to the information he'd so willingly provided had betrayed her, she managed a light, dismissive laugh.

'Just satisfying myself about your ability to provide me with the standard of living I deserve.'

'Oh, believe me, Catia——' he smiled thinly '—I can give you everything you deserve—and much more besides.'

'Good!' She decided to ignore the implied threat. 'Tell me, Nicolò, just how important was it for you to ally yourself by marriage to the family of Lorenzo? I mean . . . suppose you'd found me unattractive? Would it have made any difference to your plans?'

'You seek compliments?' His brow creased into a frown. 'I thought I'd already proved to you that I have no argument with your physical appearance.'

'But if you had?' she persisted doggedly. 'Would it still have been worth your while to marry me?'

'Of course.' He cast her an amused glance. 'Expensive clothes, make-up and a good hairdresser can work wonders with the plainest of women, but they will never add enoblement to those born without it. Your looks are an added advantage and one which I intend to enjoy to the utmost. Surely I've left you in no possible doubt about that?'

'Yes—no . . .' She gathered her thoughts with an effort and lied valiantly. 'That is, at the beginning I assumed we were both putting on an act for my grandfather and that when we returned to Italy——'

'I would leave you to your own devices?' Nicolò gave a soft laugh. 'Well, now you know differently. Has no one ever told you that availability is as good as irresistibility to most men? And as my wife, you are definitely available. Wasn't it St Paul who said it was better to marry than to burn?' There was a cold edge of irony in his voice as he asked the rhetorical question. 'In today's social climate the opportunities of burning are all too real, although not perhaps in the sense that the good saint intended.' He paused, regarding her steadfastly. 'It's a little late to have regrets. Or is it that as a lover I do not come up to your expectations?'

'No! It's not that . . .' Wildly she protested, unnerved by the expression she discerned behind the dark pupils.

'Good. Then I am glad, because a bargain is a bargain, and you cannot be the mistress of the *palazzo* unless you carry out the same service for its possessor.'

'A nominal "wife" to satisfy your other requirements of prestige and appearance isn't sufficient for you?' she asked scornfully, hurt to the quick by his contempt.

He made a dismissive gesture with one hand. 'A wife is a mistress who is always available.'

Unable to contain her appalled gasp at his heartless retort, Catia demanded coldly, 'Isn't that attitude rather feudal?'

'Of course!' His smile was the smile on the face of the tiger. 'And who better than I to know the practices of such a system? Or do you forget how badly my father suffered at the hands of the tyrant Leopoldo?'

She had momentarily forgotten. Now she felt again the uneasiness which had assailed her the first time he'd mentioned the old feud between their families, unable to suppress the shiver which trembled down her spine.

'You are cold, Catia?' She suspected that he had deliberately misread her reaction as he reached for her as if to embrace her, but she was too quick for him, stepping away from his grasp.

Ignoring his question, she faced him boldly. 'Just tell me one thing, Nicolò. Was Nonno aware of all the reasons you had for making me your wife?'

His pause was minimal, then he nodded. 'Oh, yes, but of course! I think I can safely say that he had no false impression of my motives.'

'I see.' She wished she could believe he was lying, but her heart told her that he spoke the truth.

'Do you, Catia?' This time he moved so quickly that it was impossible to evade him. His hands grasped her shoulders, drawing her into the close confines of his own body. 'I doubt it. I believe you have still a lot to learn. But let me return the question. Did your grandfather know of your desire for grandeur? Had you confided in him of your dissatisfaction with the career which you had chosen and for which he had prepared you by the investment of a great deal of his own money? Was he aware that you were lured by the promise of wealth and position to tie yourself to a man for whom you had no feelings but envy?' He shook her gently. 'Well, Catia, what do you say? Did he know the truth, or did you fool your grandfather into believing you loved me?'

Mutinously she stared into the face that had filled her dreams from that first meeting, and fed her desires. What could she say? To suggest, erroneously, that Nonno had been a party to the deception she claimed might pacify her own ego, but do untold harm to her elderly grandparent.

'Of course I deceived him!' She was pleased with the smile she was able to paint on her face. 'I fooled him completely.'

'Then I have every confidence that you can continue with your performance and fool my parents as well. As you know, they've waited a long time for me to settle down and become a family man. I wouldn't want them to be disappointed in their daughter-in-law.' He released her, leaving the sensation of his fingers to torment her sensitive skin. 'And now, *moglie mia*, since I promised you that you could choose how to spend the rest of the day, you must tell me your wishes.' The gleam in his eyes taunted her with the power of their seduction, so that she tore her gaze away, determined not to let him see her inner pain.

'Well, then,' she said lightly, deciding to play up the role she'd adopted, 'I should like to wander through the streets admiring the window displays in the shops until we reach the Rialto, then I'd like to have a light meal at one of the restaurants on the banks of the canal there...'

'Go on.' Nicolò nodded, indulging her as she paused, her eyebrows raised, awaiting his comment.

'Then I'd like to stroll back towards the Piazza san Marco and drink coffee at Florian's and listen to their orchestra play while the moon rises!' she finished triumphantly.

'The desires of a tourist,' he mocked, but not unkindly, as she finished.

'Well, that's what I am, isn't it?' she said quietly, her blue eyes reflecting the pang of sadness which assailed her. 'My father was Italian, yet for twenty-two years, all my life to date, I'd never set foot on a piece of Italian soil until yesterday. Is it so wrong of me to want to gawp and admire with all the others who've never been privileged to see the sights of Venice?' Her rounded chin came up sharply. 'If you hadn't arbitrarily brought me back here this morning I intended to explore the Basilica and the Doge's Palace. Would you prefer me to pretend an indifference to such compelling beauty?'

'As a slave to beauty myself, how can I refuse your request?' Nicolò regarded her curiously. 'If I'd supposed you were only interested in exploring buildings this morning I might have allowed you a few more moments to indulge your curiosity. But at the time I felt your desire for new experiences might have included a tour of a cabin on a cruise ship.'

'That's absurd and you know it!' She dismissed his statement with the contempt it deserved. 'Even if I was in the habit of picking up men, the ship's security system would have made unauthorised boarding impossible.'

'Then let's just say that this morning I intended to ensure that I took a personal part in your exploration of new experiences,' he returned smoothly. 'Now that aim has been accomplished I make but two provisos.'

'Yes?' Catia tensed her shoulders, wondering what terms he might order to curtail her enjoyment.

'The first is that you do not dress like a tourist.'

'Agreed.' She nodded. 'Although you do the majority of visitors a grave injustice. And the second?'

'That you remember that the day ends at midnight.'

'That sounds reasonable,' she agreed, having no real option to do otherwise, if she wanted to enjoy the remainder of her day in Venice, and was rewarded by Nicolò's triumphant smile.

All she needed to do was freshen up a little. The sleeveless pink silk dress with its deep neckline and beautifully cut skirt was elegantly understated, as befitted the Newmarket boutique from which she had bought it, and she felt no need to change again. By excellent good luck she'd managed to purchase in the *piazza* at London's Covent Garden a large square of pure Indian silk in a multi-pink Paisley design, deeply fringed in the exact colour of the dress. Fine enough to fold into her small handbag, it would emerge uncreased and, folded into a triangle, serve as a beautiful shawl should the evening breeze prove cool.

Entering their room, she'd wondered if Nicolò would make any move to stake his claim to her body again. To her relief he hadn't. It seemed that he was about to keep his word to her, and, like Cinderella, she would be able to relax until the clock struck twelve.

Nicolò was waiting in the sitting-room of the apartment when she announced herself ready to leave, casually but immaculately dressed in light trousers topped by a brown silk short-sleeved shirt with a patterned tie knotted at the neck.

Rising to his full height at her entrance, his dark gaze slowly encompassing her from the soft fall of wavy blonde hair to the low-heeled taupe sandals which graced her slim high-instepped feet, he surveyed her with critical appraisal, until she felt the colour rising to her cheeks.

'Well, do I meet with your approval, sir?' she enquired pertly, irritated by the slowness of his inspection.

'You'll do,' he commented laconically. 'Especially as it's unlikely that we shall meet anyone of any importance.'

Despite his gibe, it had been one of the happiest evenings of her life, Catia allowed several hours later as, perched self-consciously on a stool in the middle of the *piazza*, she allowed her thoughts to wander while an artist drew her portrait before an admiring crowd.

It had been Nicolò's idea that she should have her portrait drawn, and he who had selected the artist from among several plying their trade in the well-lit square beneath the star-spangled blackness of the clear sky. Now, as she heard the admiring comments of the crowd, she guessed he had chosen well and with foreknowledge of the artist's ability.

Her husband had been the perfect escort, she admitted to herself with some surprise: patiently lingering as she'd taken her fill of the elegant clothes in the numerous boutiques which lined the maze of streets between the Rialto and San Marco; waiting without adverse comment as she had gazed entranced at the shops selling carnival masks, every variety from china to fabric, bejewelled and feathered displayed in their illuminated windows; allowing her to wander down winding alleyways to walk past small pavement cafés, their outside tables garbed in pristine linen tablecloths of various hues, their cutlery and glasses gleaming under the amethyst three-lamped street lighting which added to the character of the beautiful city.

For those few hours she'd been elated, her senses replete with the sights, sounds and perfumes of the evening by the time they reached the Rialto. A momentary twinge of disappointment overtook her as she realised the restaurants were packed. She might have guessed that such a highly renowned tourist spot would be packed out early.

It was only when Nicolò had led her through one of the open-air restaurants towards an empty table right by the water's edge that she'd realised that he must have used some of the time she had kept him waiting at the *palazzo* to phone and reserve a table.

'Oh Nicolò—how lovely it is...' she'd breathed, unable to hide her spontaneous delight. Deep amber lanterns suspended from the fringe of the scarlet canopy above them had swung gently in the slight breeze, while graceful wrought-iron standards arched against the low railings, each bearing a pastel-coloured Japanese-style lantern, the low-wattage bulbs adding an extra gentle luminosity to their surroundings.

It was not yet dark, and from where she'd sat she'd been able to observe the crowds streaming across the Rialto Bridge, watch the gondolas leave from their station below the restaurant and admire the fondant-coloured buildings opposite with their thumb-shaped windows and delicately styled wrought-iron balconies.

She hadn't been hungry, but there had been no pressure put on them to leave, so she'd taken her time to enjoy a cold lobster salad followed by strawberries and ice-cream, washed down by the omnipresent *acqua minerale* and a bottle of Gambellara.

It was a good thing, she opined to herself, as she sat motionless on her perch, that she'd drunk most of the mineral water while Nicolò had enjoyed the wine. Even then there'd been some left in the bottle when they vacated the table and strolled towards the *piazza*.

It had been past eleven o'clock when he'd suggested they leave Florian's, after they'd drunk their fill of coffee and listened with pleasure to its musicians, while both tourists and Venetians sauntered around what Napoleon had nominated as 'the Drawing-Room of Europe'.

Believing they were about to make their way back to the *palazzo*, Catia had been astounded when Nicolò had led her towards the portrait artist. She had protested, but he had insisted with an imperialistic movement of his hand which had stilled her objection in mid-sentence.

A spatter of applause from the onlookers refocused her mind, drawing her attention to the easel as the artist drew back from it. Easing herself down from her perch, she moved round to view her own portrait at the same time as Nicolò came forward to pay the artist.

'Oh!' A gasp of pure astonishment escaped her lips, as she found herself looking at a stranger. Surely this beautiful creature with the clear lucid eyes of a child and the mysterious half-smile of a Mona Lisa entrapped in a long oval face, balanced by high fine cheekbones and the merest hint of a dimple in the chin, couldn't be how the artist had really seen her? She stole a sideways glance at Nicolò, anticipating his disapproval of what was clearly a chocolate-box glamorisation? But no, he was paying the fee, accepting the tissue-protected and lightly rolled parchment in its cardboard tube with every sign of gratification.

'No wonder he does such good business,' she observed mildly as Nicolò took her hand to lead her from the *piazza*, towards where the *piazzetta* led to the Riva degli Schiavoni, the broad pavement which ran along the side of the Grand Canal, 'if he turns every woman into a film-star on paper!'

Nicolò laughed at her response. 'Like most Italian males, he is openly attracted to the female face and form and instinctively finds some merit in the appearance of all women. His secret is that he regards them with the eye of a lover combined with the eye of an artist and is therefore able to bring out qualities which their contemporaries may not always perceive.' His arm sought and found her waist, drawing her close against his body, matching his stride to her shorter one, so that their legs brushed against each other. 'Do you object to what he has discovered of your nature?'

'Indeed not—it's a very flattering portrait,' she replied quickly. But deep in her heart she did object, because the artist had detected and shown her inner vulnerability. It was something she knew she had to hide from Nicolò at all costs if she was to escape from the trap into which he had led her.

Somewhere a clock chimed, sonorous and sweet, the twelve beats of midnight. As the last echo died, Nicolò stopped walking and took her purposefully into his arms, finding and covering her soft mouth with his own. For a brief moment she attempted resistance, but the pleasures of the evening were still too close, their memory too alive in her mind for her to detach herself from his masterful embrace. With an inarticulate murmur she wound her arms round his neck, standing on tiptoe, surrendering the softness of her mouth to his conquest.

He was breathing heavily when he released her, his strong body trembling with desire. 'You are a fast learner, Marchesa.' Eyes as dark as the night sky devoured her flushed face as he lifted one hand to trace the outline of her full lips with his thumb. 'Despite your earlier reluctance to meet your obligations, I believe you will grow to fulfil them very satisfactorily.'

It was only then, as Nicolò led her from the shadows to the edge of the waterfront, that Catia realised that once again he had arranged for Giovanni to bring the launch to meet them. Still shaken by her unplanned response, she allowed herself to be handed down into the comfortable cabin, drawing the filmy scarf closer round her shoulders as she shivered, knowing it was from anticipation of what lay ahead rather than the growing chill of the night air.

Nicolò didn't love her, but he did desire her. What was wrong with her? She should have felt humiliated that she was being asked to act as stand-in for a woman whose loyalties had already been pledged to another man. If it was true what Cesare Brunelli had alleged—that Nicolò had taken a wife to act as a smokescreen until Gina could obtain her divorce without scandal for the company—then she should be feeling degraded and angry. Perhaps it was the magic of Venice, or the remnants of the love she had cherished for Nicolò, or the memory of how she had felt when she had believed he truly loved her, but the anger she needed to fire her revolt against him refused to be kindled.

Despite her earlier resolution, once back at the *palazzo* she had no defences left against his purposeful seduction as he unzipped her dress with impatient hands, smoothing the soft material over her hips until it pooled at her feet, pausing to kiss her breasts as they swelled above the delicate bra which supported their fullness, before consigning it to oblivion; divesting her of her slip and briefs, lifting her in his arms and kissing the shallow dip of her navel before placing her gently on the bed and stripping off the rest of his clothes with a fervour which bordered on ecstasy.

Detaching her mind, Catia found herself entrapped yet again in a sensual spell as he touched her with the sure artistry of a man confident of his own prowess with women, until finally, surfeited with sensation and satisfaction, she drifted into sleep, her golden head pillowed on his broad chest.

Awakening as the soft light from the partly drawn blinds filtered across her face, she found that the bed beside her was empty. Languorously she stretched her hand, touching the silk sheet next to her. It felt cold. Pulling herself into a sitting position, she became aware of a light from beneath the bathroom door seconds before it opened and Nicolò re-entered the bedroom. To her surprise he was dressed in a silver-grey business suit, a dark blue tie knotted at the throat of a paler-hued shirt.

'Nicolò?' Still bemused by the dregs of sleep, she questioned his appearance as he approached her to sit down on the bed.

'I have to go to Milan on business without delay,' without preamble he made his explanation. 'There was a phone call earlier this morning. Apparently they phoned last night but Giovanni was waiting for us on the Canal and the other staff had retired.' He shrugged.

'They left a message on the answering machine, but guessed, correctly, that it might be some time before I got round to listening to it.'

'But for how long?' Carefully she masked the disappointment she felt as her eyes dwelt on the smooth masculine skin of his cheek, tough yet soft, bearing the slight scent of some astringent lotion. Last night it had been slightly abrasive with incipient beard. A prickle of awareness reawakened as she recalled the touch of it against her breast.

'A day or two... it depends on what I find awaiting me.'

What had she expected? The previous night had been a celebration of physical satisfaction in which there had been no need for anything but sexual compatibility. Bitterly she accepted that she had played the part of a concubine, attractive enough and willing enough to satisfy her master.

'Can I come with you?' she asked impulsively, knowing already what his answer would be.

'There's no time.' Brusquely he rejected her. 'I've arranged for Giovanni to take me to the mainland in a few minutes and for a car to be waiting there to take me on to Milan. All the staff will be at your beck and call to help and amuse you as you desire. You'll be in safe hands, and I have left you a good supply of *lire* on the dressing-table to indulge your desires.'

'Thank you.' She tried to smile although she felt more like crying at his obvious disdain. 'Has something gone wrong?'

'Nothing that can't be remedied.' Dark eyes alight with self-mockery scanned her pale face. 'Like a child at Christmas I allowed myself to be distracted by the novelty of a new toy, and now I must pay the price for my inattention to more serious matters.'

As she winced from the cruelty of his words, he bent to kiss her. A swift, hard, almost brutal kiss that was the dismissive farewell of the conqueror. '*Arrivederci, cara mia*—behave yourself in my absence or answer for your indiscretions on my return!'

They were the words of an employer rather than a husband, but what had she expected? To win Nicolò from Gina simply because she'd pleasured his body satisfactorily? Love was more, much more, than sexual compatibility.

Left alone in the splendid bedroom, she faced the lonely future—albeit a short one—with a devastating sense of bereavement, despite the humiliation inherent in the role she was playing. Not that she would be at a loss to occupy herself. Venice with all its delights was on her doorstep, and if she got tired of seeing old churches there were always the other islands of the lagoon she could visit.

She sighed deeply. Nicolò had scathingly referred to her as his mistress. It was an apt description. The register office ceremony had been confined to their stating that they wished to be man and wife. No vows, no promises, no morally binding declarations of love and loyalty until death them did part; and that was how it must remain until she could discover the whole truth about events in the past which had resulted in her bondage, and allow her to break the ties which bound her, because, regardless of Nicolò's plans, she had no intention of being a party to their unholy union's being consecrated in the eyes of heaven.

CHAPTER SEVEN

GAZING out over the canal, beyond the chocolate- and white-striped gondola posts with their turquoise and gold tops, towards the white arch of the Rialto Bridge with its impressive superstructure, Catia toyed with a plate of grilled prawns and their accompanying green salad. She wasn't really hungry but she'd needed a rest, and anything was better than returning to the *palazzo* and whiling the rest of the day away in splendid isolation.

Two and a half days gone and not a word from Nicolò. Not that she had expected to hear from him, she thought with weary resignation. It wasn't as if he harboured the usual feelings of a bridegroom for his new bride! Still, she couldn't help wondering how long he would have kept up the masquerade that he cared for her if she hadn't pre-empted the situation in an attempt to preserve her own pride. Not that she would have been in much doubt about his lack of feeling for her when he had announced his intention of returning to Milan without her! Any bridegroom worthy of the name, particularly an Italian one, would hardly have deserted his wife of a few days after what had appeared to be such a joyous consummation of their union. Or perhaps it was her own innocence which had endowed the occasion with a sense of fulfilment which her husband had never shared?

A pang of guilt allied to a feeling of apprehension assailed her. She should have told Nicolò of her objection to his plans for an ostentatious wedding before he'd left for Milan. That way he would have had a chance to cool down about her intended defiance. Now she was faced with the prospect of forcing a confrontation on his return—whenever that would be—and dealing with the full consequences of his hot-blooded reaction to the disruption of his plans.

'Signora Cacciatore, *come stai*?'

Her reverie broken, Catia looked up in surprise, anger tightening the muscles of her chest as Cesare Brunelli eased himself into the chair facing her. The restaurant where she had dined with Nicolò on their second evening together had been half-empty when she'd first arrived, but now, half an hour later, there were few chairs left vacant.

'*Bene*, *grazie*,' she returned his enquiry about her health with cold formality, deliberately refraining from returning the question, and deciding on the spur of the moment to discourage his presence with a lie. 'I'm just waiting for my husband to join me,' she improvised.

'Then you're in for a very long wait, I fear.' He snapped his fingers in the air, summoning the waiter, ordering a meal for himself and a carafe of wine, before returning his gleaming appraisal to Catia's stony expression. 'The last time I heard of Nicolò Cacciatore's whereabouts, he was in Milan escorting Gina Cabrini to dinner.' He glanced down at his watch. 'Of course, it's possible that he's motoring straight back this morning, but since he took the nubile Gina back to her apartment last night I think it unlikely.'

Shocked at the spasm of pain which seemed to rivet her body, Catia clenched her hands in her lap, fighting to maintain an appearance of unaltered calm.

'I'm afraid I'm not interested in your gossip, Signor Brunelli,' she said coldly.

Cesare made a clicking noise of remonstrance with his tongue. 'My dear Signora Cacciatore, you can hardly blame me for showing an interest in you. Not only is the background of your sudden union with Nicolò Cacciatore romantic and newsworthy, but you are an attractive woman, and I should hate to see you being deceived by a man who is not only your superior in age but experience as well.'

Silence was golden, but how could she sit there and allow Nicolò to be maligned by this unprincipled gossip-monger, however ambivalent her own feelings towards her husband? The only thing in Brunelli's favour was that at last he had stopped his irritating habit of addressing her as Marchesa. Abandoning caution, she kept her voice under control with an effort. 'My husband is in Milan on business, and my reason for pretending otherwise was merely an attempt to be polite. Since you can't take a hint, I must ask you outright to find another table.'

'Impossible, I'm afraid,' her tormentor returned cheerfully. 'There doesn't appear to be one vacant, and here comes my order.'

'Good, I hope you enjoy it!' Catia reached beneath the table for her handbag, determined to leave, despite the fact she'd hardly touched a mouthful of her meal, and her legs still ached from her morning's tour of some of the city's treasure houses.

'Do you want a picture?'

'Of myself sharing a table with you?' she asked scornfully, deliberately misunderstanding his meaning. 'I'd be ashamed to be seen in such company!'

Cesare smiled, impervious to her insult. 'Of your husband and Gina Cabrini dining together. Or, if you prefer it, of the two of them entering the door to her apartment. I'm afraid the second one isn't very good, because the lady attempted to hide her face, but the Cabrini legs are quite unmistakable to those in the know.'

A rising tide of despair seemed to catch Catia by the throat. Fool that she was, she'd taken Nicolò's explanation for his sudden summons to Milan at face value. Wasn't it bad enough that he was carrying on a clandestine affair without her humiliation being made public? Anger gave her the strength to keep her composure.

'So?' She rose to her feet, pushing her chair back. 'You told me yourself that my husband and Gina Cabrini are long-time friends. What more natural than that they should dine together? And as for escorting her back to her home, why not? My husband is a gentleman.'

'A man, certainly!' Cesare taunted. 'And one whom the ladies find extremely attractive. I suppose it is possible he went back with her for a cup of bedtime cocoa—but if so he took a very long time to drink it. Two hours later my contact gave up watching the place and went back to bed.'

'And I'm supposed to believe that it's a pure coincidence that you saw me sitting here and decided to acquaint me with your suspicions?' she countered haughtily.

'Of course not,' Cesare responded smoothly. 'I've been combing the tourist spots of Venice since dawn in an attempt to wise you up to what's going on behind your back. Call it an act of charity, before the news reverberates round Venice.'

'Call it an act of slander!' Catia retorted fiercely. 'Publish those photographs with any imputation of misbehaviour and my husband's lawyers will sue you!'

'Come, come,' he chided. 'Have you never heard the saying that all publicity is good publicity? And that the truth is always an impeachable defence to the accusation of libel? Besides, there will be plenty of photographs of them together tomorrow night, will there not? All seemingly innocent and above board, with the beautiful and intriguing new wife of Nicolò Cacciatore playing chaperon. Poor Giuseppe Cabrini—he'll be gnashing his teeth in frustration!'

'Tomorrow night?' The words escaped her lips before she had the presence of mind to bite her tongue into silence.

'Oh, dear, you didn't know.' Cesare Brunelli's face assumed an expression of guilt so false that Catia cursed herself for falling into the trap he had set her.

She shrugged her shoulders, furious with Nicolò for neglecting to inform her of any social arrangements he had made and in which she was apparently being included. 'Now I think of it, he did say something about a dinner party,' she ad libbed. 'But I'm afraid my mind was on other things and I didn't pay much attention.'

'Obviously.' Impertinent eyes mocked her attempt to cover her ignorance. 'Cacciatore's performance as a lover must indeed be as mesmerising as reputed if it made you confuse one of the social highlights of Venice with a simple dinner party.'

She heard his low chuckle of disbelieving laughter and knew that she must leave while she still had control over her legs. Pride forbade that she should question her insolent companion further. Nicolò was the one who owed her an explanation and it was Nicolò who should provide it. Grabbing her handbag, she pushed her chair back and got to her feet before Brunelli had guessed her purpose.

Instantly he was on his feet, the epitome of Italian courtesy, withdrawing a small card from one of his pockets, and thrusting it imperiously at her.

'Wait! The time may yet come when you need a friend. If so, you can contact me on one of these numbers.'

She should have ignored him, but some sixth sense incited her to accept the card and slip it into the outside pocket of her bag as she turned from him.

'*Signora*.' It was the head waiter who approached her as she weaved through the tables towards the pavement. 'Was the meal not to your liking?'

'On the contrary, it was excellent,' she retorted frostily. 'It was the company which offended me.' She indicated the still smiling figure of the journalist. 'Signor Brunelli will settle my bill.'

It wasn't much of a revenge when what she would have liked to do was to empty a bowl of hot minestrone over his smug head, but that would hardly have endeared her to Nicolò if the result of her action had been her being arrested for actual bodily harm, and, resentful as she was about the way Nicolò had tricked her into marrying him, she couldn't ignore the fact that both her own and her grandfather's future depended on his bounty.

So Brunelli had told her the truth about Nicolò and Gina Cabrini. Only as she felt angry tears rise to the surface of her eyes did she realise just how much she'd been hoping, against all hope, that he'd been lying or mistaken.

There was a bitter taste on her tongue as she turned blindly down a side-alley, intent on putting as much distance as possible between herself and the brutal Brunelli. The journalist had no conscience, no qualms...but what motive could he have in pursuing her with the proof of Nicolò's infidelities? Was he hoping she'd create a scene and make good copy for his column?

As for the forthcoming social event which Gina Cabrini would attend...how dared Nicolò forbear to warn her about it? Would he have been so devoid of decency if she hadn't lied about her own reasons for becoming his wife? she wondered. Yet how could she have lived out a lie after hearing what she had before they'd left for the airport?

Angrily she brushed the back of her hand against her eyes as she felt the tears gather. Nonno! Her misery deepened as she thought about her grandfather and Aunt Becky. Only yesterday she'd sent them a letter telling them how beautiful Venice was and how she was enjoying herself discovering its treasures. Deliberately she'd refrained from mentioning the fact that she was spending the time by herself! What had she been trying to protect—her own vanity, or the elderly couple's peace of mind? she wondered ruefully. Her grandfather had enough to worry about, having been blackmailed into agreeing to an arranged marriage; the minimum she could do was spare him the pain of discovering that she had found out the truth. At least, she qualified, until she'd found a way to extricate herself without repercussions.

If only her grandfather hadn't been elevated to the ranks of the non-existent Italian nobility, she reflected bitterly. If it hadn't been for that and the publicity surrounding it, Nicolò would probably never have known of her existence, and she'd still be back in London doing a job she loved, instead of walking the streets of Venice, alone with her anguish.

Turning a corner, she stopped walking with a gasp of surprise and pleasure as she found herself in a small square dominated by an exquisite church, its walls marbled and gleaming in renaissance splendour, its cupolas glowing with the light of the reflected sun.

She'd been walking through a warren of canals and narrow walkways behind the Rialto, intent only on getting as far away from Cesare Brunelli as she could, hardly expecting to find such a treasure so far off the beaten tourist track.

Close by, her eye caught a photographer's window. Drawn by some unknown instinct, she walked across to it and found herself gazing at a variety of photographs of brides and grooms. Could fate really have been so cruel? Anguish tore at her heart. Yes, it could. Purely by chance she'd discovered Santa Maria dei Miracoli, the church where Nicolò had proposed they make their vows before God, thus binding her to him with bonds stronger than any civil celebrant could apply.

And if she had agreed—then what? she demanded of herself fiercely. All she would have had to look forward to was a life of comparative physical luxury and emotional deprivation. She should turn away, leave the church with its inner secrets intact. Because she would never see its interior as a bride.

The resolution was a good one but outmatched by her curiosity. With everyone at lunch, the square was deserted. Finding an open door, Catia stepped inside, breathing a sigh of delight when she saw what awaited her. It was indeed like stepping into the jewel box from which it got its colloquial name. Sunlight streamed through the windows, sending piercing rays of light glinting off the arched golden ceiling, from which gazed down the portraits of what she could only presume to be holy men over the ages.

Everywhere she looked there seemed to be gold and marble—too much to absorb in only a few seconds. Quietly she slipped into one of the empty pews. Here at last, in front of the towering altar with its picture of the Virgin Mary, was the coolness, peace and quiet she needed.

Impossible to say how long she sat there gazing at the splendour surrounding her, or how much time she wasted afterwards strolling along the banks of canals and over bridges, stopping every now and then to look into shop windows, marvelling at the variety and style of goods on display. She'd forgotten to put her watch on that morning, but from the position of the sun in the sky she guessed the evening was approaching fast.

Another lonely night of misery ahead of her. She sighed as she walked across the graceful bridge which led to the *palazzo*, then, making her way through the gate into the garden, caught her breath in surprise as the tall figure of her husband rose from the parapet seat and came forward to greet her.

'Nicolò! I didn't expect you back until tomorrow!' Horrified at the instinctive rush of pleasure she felt at seeing him, she felt the warm blood rush to her cheeks.

His dark eyes swept swiftly over her pale trousers and light cotton top.

'Blushing, Catia? Can it be that you're pleased to see me—or confused because my unannounced return has interrupted your plans for the evening?'

'I wasn't expecting you...' She stumbled over the words.

'Clearly.' He gazed at her thoughtfully. 'I apologise for intruding into your life again so soon when it's apparent that you find my appearance so unsettling.'

Before she could respond to his taunt he moved swiftly to take her into his arms with the authority and purpose his role in her life commanded, and, tipping her chin, kissed her lengthily and sweetly.

'Do I read reproach in your lovely eyes, Catia?' He smiled cruelly as she pulled away from his embrace, unwilling for him to probe the windows of her soul and see its misery.

'Come.' Unabashed by her silence, he took her hand and led her back into the *palazzo* and up the magnificent staircase to their apartment, his grip so determined that it was just short of painful. 'Let us see if the gift I've brought you back from Milan will return the smile to your lips.'

Wordlessly she allowed him to lead her upstairs to their apartment, where he handed her a black and gold wrapped box emblazoned with a famous designer's name.

Intrigued, she held her bitterness in restraint as she carefully unwrapped it and drew forth an evening dress. Simply cut with a wide, low neck, sleeveless and with a draped skirt, its effectiveness lay in the material. Over a foundation of deep gold silk was a layer of bronze and gold silk fibres woven into an open basket-weave pattern, a crunchy honeycomb which glistened and sparkled in the fading rays of the sun as they reached through the open balcony window.

'It's beautiful, Nicolò,' she said honestly, a pang of anguish for what might have been threatening to destroy the composure of her carefully controlled features.

'Good.' He nodded smugly. 'I imagine you would have preferred to go shopping for your own dress, but with time so short I decided to surprise you. There won't be a woman in the room to compare with you tomorrow night.'

'Tomorrow?' Catia's heart skipped a beat. Cesare Brunelli had indeed told her the truth. 'Are we entertaining, then?' she asked, assuming an expression of innocent enquiry.

'I should have told you earlier...' Nicolò made a dismissive movement with his hands. 'But there were always other priorities, and I left in such a rush the other morning that it went out of my mind. Gina Cabrini is putting on a fashion show here in the ballroom, using some of the stock from her fashion boutiques. It's an annual occurrence and, since the proceeds go to charity, I could hardly call it off at the last moment.'

'I see.' Catia digested the information for a few seconds, as a half-formed idea made her clutch at a slender straw. 'Is that why you had to go to Milan? To see Gina and finalise the arrangements?'

'*Santo cielo*, *no*!' He threw back his dark head with a bark of laughter. 'Everything was arranged months ago, as far as I'm concerned. If any last-minute problems had arisen they would have been Gina's responsibility.' The amusement left his face as suddenly as it had appeared, to be replaced with a scowl. 'No, my summons to Milan involved a security leak about one of the new designs we're marketing in the USA.'

'I see.' She turned away, guessing from the tone of his voice that he was not prepared to discuss his business problems with her and determining not to risk being snubbed if she followed her natural instincts to question him further about them. In the role she'd decided to play there would be no place for wifely concern.

'How did you know my size?' She touched the delicate, expensive fabric of the dress, seeing no size on the designer label, but instinctively aware that it would fit her to perfection.

'When I realised how little time there was I phoned the *palazzo*, and since you weren't available I asked Maria to tell me the size of your dresses in the wardrobe.'

'Clever.' She forced her lips into a smile. But still the demon that tormented her would not be put to rest.

'It's a beautiful dress,' she persisted. 'Did it come from one of Gina's boutiques?'

There was the slightest pause while his narrowed gaze assessed her guileless expression.

'As a matter of fact, yes, it did. Is that a problem?'

Catia shrugged. 'Should it be?'

'Only if it were to be paraded in front of tomorrow's assembly with a price-tag attached. But you can rest assured that won't be the case. The dress is a one-off model.'

'How clever of Gina to estimate my taste so accurately when she's never met me.' Catia cast overtly admiring eyes over the garment, but inside she was fuming. How dared he ask his mistress to choose a dress for his wife?

Nicolò raised a lazy eyebrow, as the gleam in his eyes behind the fan of dark lashes told her he was not deceived by her air of insouciance.

'The credit for that is mine, not Gina's,' he informed her softly. 'The only part Gina played in the selection of your dress was to authorise her chief outlet in Milan to send a dozen or so of their couturier models to my apartment for my approval.'

'Before or after you made love?'

The words were out before she could stop them, her hand rising in her throat as if to protect it as Nicolò took a step towards her, his expression thunderous.

'Never let me hear you ask such a question again! You knew the score when you agreed to become my wife. You admitted it with your own tongue. What I choose to do with my life outside our relationship has nothing to do with you. As for Gina Cabrini, if you can't speak of her with respect then I prefer you don't speak of her at all. Is that understood?'

For one terrifying moment she thought he was going to strike her as he towered above her. In the circumstances discretion was certainly the better part of valour, she determined hastily.

'That's fine by me, but you may have greater difficulty in stilling other people's tongues. From what I've heard, the whole of Venice regards the two of you as inseparable.' Ignoring the dangerous narrowing of his eyes, she forced her voice into conversational mode, as she eyed the dress with admiration. 'Obviously a lady of many talents, your childhood friend.'

'I'm delighted you approve of my choice.' The coolness of his tone belied the spark of anger which darkened his pupils to obsidian.

'Oh, I do.' Carefully she took the dress to the built-in wardrobe and hung it on a padded hanger. 'And I'm sure your friend will be equally gratified that I will be providing a living, walking, talking advertisement for her fashion empire.'

'I'm sure she will, if you choose to disclose the fact, *mia cara*, but the evening's main purpose is to raise money for charity, not to publicise a chain of high-class fashion boutiques which are already renowned throughout Italy and France.'

There was no disguising the impatient tone of his reply or the betraying manner in which a muscle twitched beside his mouth as he clamped his jaw. Was she at last beginning to get beneath his skin? Did he really believe she was going to be grateful for such small crumbs from his table when he was deceiving her so shamelessly?

'Oh, a worthy cause!' She tossed him a warm smile that stretched her acting ability to its limit. 'Now that's something I shall really enjoy supporting. Of course, I shall have to buy some evening sandals and an evening bag. Oh, and perhaps I should arrange to have my hair dressed specially... I wouldn't want to disgrace you.'

She was aware of the silence behind her as, after spending as much time as possible arranging the hanging of the dress in the wardrobe, she turned reluctantly to meet Nicolò's thoughtful appraisal.

'Neither should I wish you to.' His brooding gaze stripped through the veneer of her defiance. 'But there is little danger of that. On the surface you had little to offer a man in my position when I first met you, but I have the eye of a connoisseur, Catia *mia*, and perceived the potential lurking beneath your unexploited exterior.'

Her gasp of pain died in her throat as he extended his hand and grasped her chin with lean fingers. 'Despite your venal leanings, you possess the fine bones and thin skin of a true aristocrat, Marchesa,' he said softly. 'My parents will be enchanted by your outward appearance at least and feel gratified when you walk down the aisle of the Golden Jewel Box, in front of a church full of witnesses, to become my golden wife in the sight of heaven.'

It was the opportunity she had been waiting for, and a deep fury encouraged her to confront him while her blood still raced through her veins in response to the proprietorial air with which he'd treated her.

'They'll have to wait until Venice sinks before that day!' she stormed, wrenching herself from his hold. 'I've no intention of making a spectacle of myself to publicise the firm of Cacciatore Auto Design. As far as I'm concerned, we've already achieved what we both wanted. There's no purpose in another meaningless ceremony.'

'Not meaningless, Catia.' The grimness of Nicolò's expression increased the rhythm of her heartbeat as adrenalin surged into her nervous system. 'The ceremony in England was to allay the fears of your grandfather, lest I change my mind once we were out of his jurisdiction and decide not to make an honest woman of you, as the saying goes.' He smiled without humour. 'Although in your case honesty is a matter of degree, is it not? Perhaps he guessed I should discover the true nature lurking behind the façade of innocence you manage to convey. Whatever his reason, it was nothing but a legal formality, and one which my parents will not recognise. My father, in particular, has waited a long time to see his only son marry. For many years if you remember, he was childless until his first wife died, and now he's in his eighties—a man of his generation. Unless we consecrate our union in church, he will regard you as being my mistress, not my wife.'

'So?' She lifted a slim shoulder in dismissal, clutching at the straw which might yet make him change his mind about taking her in payment of a debt. 'Their opinion doesn't concern me, and there's no way you can force me to make an exhibition of myself by taking part in a religious ceremony against my will.'

'You intend to defy my wishes?' His lustrous eyes burned with anger. 'Instead of my wife, you prefer to be regarded as my mistress by my family?'

'That's their problem, not mine! I've stopped living in the Dark Ages.'

'And your children? Are you content for their grandparents to regard them as bastards?' A dark fury clotted his vocal cords so that his voice shook.

'Children?' Her eyes widened in shock. Since she'd discovered Nicolò's deceit her thoughts had been concentrated solely on extricating herself from a loveless union. The idea that such a union should bear fruit was untenable, yet she had no means at her disposal of preventing such an event if nature willed it. It added a further dimension to her problem that she hadn't even considered, so great had been the extent of her trauma.

'But of course,' Nicolò confirmed smoothly. 'It was always my intention from the moment I saw you that the bloodline of Cacciatore and Lorenzo should fuse to become one. *Allora*...' He came towards her, his amorous intentions written in every line of his prepossessing face, every lazy movement of his superb body. 'I wish you luck in explaining to your grandfather your reasons for denying him the pleasure of hearing you make your vows, but, if you think your decision to deny me the church's blessing will keep me from enjoying what I have bought, then you are sadly mistaken.'

Panic seized Catia, and she held out her arms stiffly in front of her in an abortive attempt to ward him off. She'd wanted his love, not just the sexual satisfaction of his body, but it seemed she had no choice, for he overcame her resistance, his mouth searing hers like a tongue of fire, seductive and demanding. Torn by ambivalent feelings, she found that her feeble struggles were no match for Nicolò's resolution, and in moments he'd lifted and carried her to the bed, where to her shame she felt her being alter in instant response to the gradually descending embrace of his strong, virile body.

There was no room for logic now as, despite her emotional pain, she became obsessed with his essence, directing her hands to tangle in the sable silkiness of his thick hair, to pull him even closer until his weight pressed her into the softness of the bed and she became a total victim of the sweet relentless passion that flamed between them.

When he eased himself away to strip his magnificent body with swift, economical movements, she could only stare at him with bewildered eyes, her heart thudding with expectation until he returned to straddle her, peeling her garments from her with gentle purposeful fingers, caressing her revealed nudity with the touch of almost fearful appreciation as if he knew how tender were the tips of her tumescent breasts as they strained towards his hand.

Eyes half shuttered, he wrought his magic until she became totally subjugated by the demands of her aroused body, begging him silently to possess her and give her solace.

In the aftermath of passion she lay alone where he left her, slow, silent tears taking the path of least resistance to be absorbed by the silk pillowcase. She had no one but herself to blame. In his view she had elected to be his mistress—or *one* of his mistresses, she allowed bitterly—and he had left her in no doubt as to what that would mean during the time she was compelled to stay in Italy in an attempt to discover the nature of the debt of honour her grandfather owed.

CHAPTER EIGHT

THE music played, the models strutted and pirouetted down the catwalk and Catia sat silent, her head turned away from the elegant figure of Nicolò seated beside her immaculate in a light-jacketed tuxedo, hands clasped in her lap, her eyes fixed on their manoeuvres, seeing but not registering the display of elegant garments.

She had seen little of her husband during the evening which had followed their heated lovemaking. Only when they'd both been changing for the evening had there been any conversation between them, and that had revolved around what Nicolò saw as her duties for the entertainment the following evening. He had been cool and distant, clearly angered by her defiance, his outrage evident in every movement of his lean agile body. Neither, of course, had he mentioned dining with Gina. If it had been innocent, surely there was no reason why he shouldn't? But he'd remained adamantly silent about the way he'd spent his time away from her, presumably to protect Gina's reputation rather than out of any consideration for her own position in his household!

After dinner on the terrace, where the conversation had been formal and coldly polite, Nicolò had retired to the offices above and she'd seen nothing further of him until he'd joined her in bed at midnight.

To her relief, he'd made no attempt to touch her and she'd lain awake long into the night listening to his light, steady breathing beside her, her heart breaking as she remembered the brief happiness she'd enjoyed in the fool's paradise of Suddingham. Suppose she'd hadn't overheard her grandfather's confession? Would Nicolò have continued to act out the part of devoted lover? She doubted it.

Once Gina Cabrini was free of her unwanted husband, the Italian woman would doubtless be available to Nicolò on any terms he wished, without causing a scandal within his beloved company! At that time the need for subterfuge would have ended. All she had achieved by her unwitting eavesdropping had been to preserve a little of her own pride.

By the time they'd finished breakfast, preparations for the evening had been well under way in the ballroom. The stage and catwalk were being erected with practised ease, gilt and velvet chairs being produced by a small army of workmen from some hidden store within the basement of the *palazzo*, and long tables being put into place ready to be clothed and adorned with glass and silver when the dust had settled.

Nicolò, dressed in jeans and a dark roll-neck cotton sweater, was directing operations, but there was no place for her in that mêlée of activity, and she'd been glad of the excuse to leave the *palazzo* to search for shoes and handbag and arrange for her hair to be done.

She'd taken her time, choosing to have a light snack at a *tavola calda*, enjoying a plate of *zucchini ripieni*, standing at the counter forking the delicious stuffed marrow into her mouth surrounded by dozens of Venetians doing the same thing, as if she had lived in the city all her life.

By the time she returned to the *palazzo*, bag and sandals duly bought, her hair elaborately styled, lifted, twisted and sprayed into a crown of gold on her neat head, everything was ready. The models had arrived, tall, skinny girls, their facial bones sharp and chiselled, their profiles the type beloved of the camera lens.

All except one. It took but a split-second for Catia to realise that the exception was Gina Cabrini. Her fingers had tightened on the bag which contained her purchases as she cursed the impulse which had made her dress casually in pink cotton trousers and baggy sleeveless top, because Gina Cabrini was absolutely gorgeous, her simple lime-green shift dress enhancing the full thrust of her breasts and revealing shapely calves beneath its knee-length hem.

A stab of pure jealousy lanced through Catia's heart. If she could have crept unseen up the stairs to the apartment she would have done so rather than confront the woman she saw as her rival, when she was so unprepared for the meeting; but fate was against her, as Nicolò emerged from a small crowd of artisans to take her by the arm.

'Catia! At last! I thought you must have got lost!' But there was no real concern in his voice as he smiled down at her. 'Now I see from your elaborate hairstyle where you must have spent most of your time.'

'Do you like it?' She met his gaze defensively, her inferiority complex running high.

'I prefer it lying loose on my pillow,' he taunted her softly. 'But for public display it's quite stunning. And now I want you to meet Gina. I think she was beginning to believe that you were a figment of my imagination.'

Believe or hope? Catia wondered sadly as she allowed herself to be escorted across the room.

Close to, Gina was still stunning. Large hazel eyes, deep-set in a thick creamy skin beneath flaring dark brows and fringed with sable lashes, sparkled a welcome which had every appearance of being genuine. A wide, full mouth lifted in a smile as she extended her hand in greeting.

'I feel I should apologise for disrupting your honeymoon, but the invitations had already been sent out before Nicolò sprung his surprise on us!' Gina cast a reproving look at him that didn't quite conceal the affection behind the rebuke.

'Not at all.' Summoning all the grace she could muster, Catia took the other woman's cool hand. 'In fact I'm looking forward to the show. I believe I have you to thank for the dress Nicolò brought back from Milan for me?'

'Not me personally.' Smoothly Gina denied the supposition. 'I merely arranged for Nicolò to be presented with a choice. Having known him for a long time, I'm convinced that his taste in women's clothing is excellent. I hope you weren't disappointed?'

'Of course she wasn't!' Nicolò took it on himself to reply, his tone smugly confident. 'When you see her tonight you will understand why.'

It was at that point that Catia had made her excuses and left them together, Gina's attestation to a long association with Nicolò ringing in her ears. Was this her way of making her role in Nicolò's life clear? Or had she felt that she, Catia, might resent her clothes being chosen by another woman?

The irony was that in any other situation she would have welcomed advice from the Italian girl—or was woman a better title? Because Gina was closer to Nicolò's age, she suspected, although with her dark, short curly hair and voluptuous figure she could have passed for a teenager until one saw the lines of strain round her fine eyes when the smile died.

Now, watching what seemed an endless parade of exquisite clothes, Catia allowed her mind to drift back to the start of the evening's entertainment, when she'd sat beside Nicolò on the rostrum as he'd welcomed the assembled guests. It had been an ordeal for her, conscious as she'd been of all those critical eyes fixed on her as Nicolò had referred to her as his wife, and she had blushed at the round of applause which had greeted his announcement, relieved when she'd been able to leave the rostrum to take her seat on one of the velvet chairs beside the catwalk.

Gina had been right about Nicolò's taste, she admitted, allowing her fingers to caress the material of her dress. It was breathtakingly lovely and fitted her to perfection. She'd been aware that the covetous glances she had collected from some of the other women, and the admiring looks of the men, had been due to its subtle opulence.

A murmur of admiration and a smattering of applause greeted what had to be the culmination of the event—a wedding-dress in ivory satin and lace. Catia's heart seemed to turn over as she lifted one hand to finger the dangling gold ornament which graced her left ear in a betraying gesture of nervousness. If Nicolò had had his way she would soon be wearing such a dress. Everything inside her revolted at the idea. Whatever pressures Nicolò tried to bring to bear on her over the forthcoming days—and she was sure these would be multiple—she would continue to defy him. He could hardly beat her into submission, could he?

The show was over, the assembly stretching their legs and making for the buffet, the women eagerly exchanging their views, the men grimacing at each other as they realised the pressure which was about to descend on their bank accounts.

Taking the opportunity of slipping away from his side while Nicolò was congratulating Gina, Catia made her way towards the laden tables, accepting a glass of champagne from a passing waiter and sipping it gratefully.

'Congratulations, Signora Cacciatore—tonight you look more like a queen than a *marchesa*!'

She'd recognise that voice anywhere! Catia turned a disdainful face towards Cesare Brunelli as he came to stand in front of her. 'You again?' she asked, not attempting to hide the dislike in her voice.

'I'm a very popular person,' he confirmed, apparently not disquieted by her disapproval. 'All these people are only too anxious to receive the publicity I can give them.'

'Then they're welcome to it. My husband and I can do without it.'

'Ah, you still wish me not to publish the photograph of your husband with the nubile Gina taken outside her apartment?'

Catia shrugged her contempt, although her heart was thudding in her chest as if it were trying to break loose. Regardless of what Nicolò had done to her, it wasn't in either of their interests for such a photograph to be published. She had no wish for her humiliation to be made public; neither would her situation be improved by the worsening of Nicolò's temper. 'I doubt anyone would find it of interest, even if it did exist.'

'Oh, it exists all right.' A hand slid into the pocket of his dinner-jacket and withdrew the evidence.

One horrified glance confirmed what he'd alleged. Despite the raised handbag, the woman was definitely Gina and Nicolò's arm was round her shoulders, his profile turned towards her, the expression caring.

'They're old friends,' she ad libbed, wondering why she felt as if her heart were encased in ice. Had she ever doubted that the meeting had taken place? 'Nicolò told me he'd been to see her to arrange for a selection of dresses to be made available for me.'

'An endearing explanation.' His mouth twisted in a smile. 'My readers will find it charming. As charming as I find your dress.' His sharp eyes followed the lines of her body. 'A classy dress for a very classy lady. If Nicolò Cacciatore's intention was to add breeding to his indifferent pedigree than he couldn't have chosen a better wife to be the mother of his children. You may only be the granddaughter of a *marchese*, but your blue blood shows, *signora*.'

'How dare you be so insulting?' Catia's eyes flashed fury as her temper got the better of her at the journalist's percipient realisation of her role. 'Invitation or not, if you can't keep your vile insinuations to yourself, I'll have you thrown out!'

'*Che cosa capita*?' Nicolò's cool and authoritative voice from somewhere behind her made Catia bite her lip in chagrin. The last thing she wanted was a showdown between these two men in such a public place.

'Nothing,' she said in a subdued voice. 'Nothing's the matter. I misunderstood something that Signor Brunelli said, that's all.'

'Brunelli?' Nicolò's look was scathing as it dwelt on the other man's face. 'Ah, yes. The man who earns his living by reporting rumour and calumny. Have you been insulting my wife?' His arm encircled her waist, drawing her closer to him. 'Because if you have——'

Brunelli's low laughter dismissed the allegation. 'Of course not. Your wife and I are the greatest of friends, are we not, Catia?' His simian eyes mocked her as he tilted his head to one side, appraising her pale face. 'In fact you have me to thank for keeping her company in your absence, else the poor girl wouldn't have known what to do with her time. Fortunately, I was at a bit of a loose end myself, so I was able to amuse her with some of the gossip you dismiss so scurrilously.'

'*Bugiardo*!' Nicolò's arm tightened cruelly around Catia's waist, as Cesare Brunelli's expression lost all sign of humour.

'Nicolò, please...' she whispered. 'People are beginning to look at us.' Somehow she had to distract him before he lashed out at Cesare Brunelli. He had no idea of the incriminating photograph in the other man's pocket. As it was there was an even chance of it not being published, but if Nicolò should strike out at the journalist, as appeared possible, she sensed that the latter would delight in embarrassing them all publicly.

'A liar, am I?' Brunelli took a step backwards but the smile had returned to his face. 'There is a restaurateur by the Rialto Bridge who will prove otherwise. Not only will he confirm that your wife and I lunched there yesterday, but also that she asked—no, insisted—that I should pay her bill.' He turned his mocking gaze to Catia's frozen countenance. 'True or false, Marchesa?'

For a moment she hesitated, wondering how to answer such a loaded question, then Nicolò said quietly, 'Well, Catia, did this man pay for your lunch?'

'Yes, but...' She bit her lip in frustration. 'It's not the way it sounds...'

'Then I apologise for calling you a liar.' Nicolò's fingers dug painfully into her waist as he made the formal apology, through tight lips. 'It seems you are correct in accusing me of neglecting my wife. I shall have to see it doesn't happen again.'

'Nicolò...' As Cesare Brunelli smirked and turned away, Catia placed a shaking hand on her husband's arm, alarm piercing her spirit at her husband's expression. 'I can explain...'

'Of course you can—and will—but later, *cara mia*.' With an impatient gesture he shrugged off her restraining fingers. 'It seems you need to learn discretion, and it will be my pleasure to teach you, but not in front of all these strangers.'

He moved away, leaving her alone, anger and despair fighting a lonely battle in her heart. Observing a few interested glances turned in her direction, she assumed a nonchalant smile, moving gracefully towards another waiter and exchanging her empty glass for a full one.

At least if there was to be a reckoning with Nicolò later that night she would make him tell her the truth, the whole truth! Taking a sip of champagne, she felt a wave of warmth tremble through her, suffusing her face with unwonted colour as she recalled Brunelli's careless allegation that Nicolò had married her to add quality to his bloodline.

Pain clutched at her heart as she remembered an incident on the night of the syndicate party in Newmarket, when Nicolò had been discussing with her his plans to buy a racehorse and she had laughingly taunted him with his lack of knowledge about bloodstock. She could hear his voice in her mind as if it had been yesterday. 'On the contrary, I have already learned from Richard a good deal more than you suppose. For instance, I am fully aware that the breeding of the mare is the vital factor in determining quality of the progeny...'

It was further evidence that Cesare Brunelli had been spot-on with his diagnosis of her role in Nicolò's plans. *Marchesas*, especially those who were unaware of their claim to nobility and who could be easily manipulated by a clever and resourceful man, must be pretty thin on the ground, she accorded bitterly, as a wave of faintness caused her to clutch at a nearby pillar. Suppose she was already pregnant? Such a predicament would hideously complicate her plans for extricating herself from the mess she was in.

There was no way she could stand where she was, trying to behave in a civilised way, while her whole life was disintegrating around her. Taking a deep breath to steady herself, she managed somehow to weave her way towards the garden, slipping through the open doors and gaining the sanctuary of the dimly lit terrace without incident. Later perhaps, when the crowds within had satisfied their appetites and thirsts, they would spill out and invade the space she had claimed for herself; but for the moment she was alone.

It was only when she'd curled up on the balustrade seat that she realised she had been mistaken in her assumption of solitude as a figure rose from the swinging seat and walked across towards her.

Gina Cabrini was the last person, barring Brunelli, whom she wished to see, but there was something about the other woman's face, a look of almost unbearable tension, which touched her soft heart.

Dressed in a bare-shouldered gown of deep crimson satin, its high line reminiscent of the Empress Josephine, Gina's beauty did nothing to alleviate the pain in Catia's heart.

'Like me, you find the crowds oppressive?' The Italian woman stood, hands on the balustrade, staring out over the Canal.

'A little,' Catia said from between dry lips. 'But it's been a very interesting evening.'

'Yes.' Gina sighed, then swayed slightly, her fingers clutching at the stone.

'Are you feeling faint?' Concern brought Catia to her feet as she saw the other woman's pallor. 'Here, sit down.'

'It's nothing...' Gina tried to smile but the tiny quirk of her lips came to nothing as she stumbled and then obeyed Catia's command. 'It's probably just the excitement...' Her voice trailed away as she buried her head in her hands.

It was at that moment that Catia knew. Divine inspiration allied to the sudden understanding of the implication of the clothes Gina had been wearing—the shift dress this morning and now the Empire-line gown which carefully concealed her waist.

'Or pregnancy?' she suggested softly, and was rewarded by the sight of Gina's large hazel eyes lifted towards her, the accuracy of her guess clearly confirmed in their expression: half relief, half anxiety.

'Nicolò told you?'

'You asked him not to?' Her blood turned to ice, Catia could hardly bring herself to ask the question.

'No, no...I preferred that he did.' Gina's hands clasped together so strongly that her knuckles gleamed white in the semi-darkness. 'I thought I saw someone take a photograph of us as we went back to my apartment, and I'm sure we were being watched in the restaurant. I wanted you to know the truth, in case one of the papers published something about us. Ever since I left my husband I've been a target for reporters. Nicolò wanted to keep it a secret until he could take some positive action but I'm glad he changed his mind.'

'What exactly did he propose to do?' Catia asked calmly. Could it really be she, talking so calmly to her husband's beloved? How long would this unnatural calm last, she wondered, and what would she do when it retreated?

'He was going to talk to Giuseppe, my husband, and tell him everything.' She gave a tremulous laugh. 'It's ironic, isn't it? All these months Giuseppe's been trying to trap me with my lover so that he can disgrace and divorce me, and now it's only a matter of weeks before the evidence of my "infidelity" is plain for all to see!'

Nicolò's child. Gina Cabrini was carrying Nicolò's child. So much for the noble blood he had desired for his son or daughter! But what now? Obviously he didn't intend to recognise Gina's child as his own. At least not officially, since he'd made it quite clear the previous evening that he wanted to consolidate his marriage to herself. The ache in Catia's heart deepened. An unofficial liaison, then, but one which, with the presence of a child to bind it, would be long and lasting.

'I suppose the outcome of your divorce is a foregone conclusion now,' she hazarded tentatively, wishing she could hate Gina but finding it strangely impossible. From the desperation apparent on Gina's face, a child had not been on the immediate agenda for their future.

Dully she nodded. 'Giuseppe has always wanted children. He will welcome me back, if not with open arms, at least with a degree of tolerance, even though he no longer cares about me. We are still husband and wife.'

It wasn't the answer Catia had expected, and for a moment she was stunned.

'You'll go back to your husband?' she asked, unable to mask her astonishment.

'Wouldn't you, in the circumstances?' Gina asked impassively. 'What real alternative do I have if I want my child to be brought up with two parents?' She rose carefully to her feet. 'I should apologise for discussing my problems with you.' She smiled wanly. 'Nicolò has stood by me since I told him I had conceived. In fact I don't know what I would have done without his support.' She smoothed the crimson satin carefully over her hips and for a brief moment the fact of her pregnancy was obvious.

Six months, Catia thought bleakly. Gina must have carried her child for at least that period. So it wasn't a recent occurrence. Surely Nicolò would have known about it long before he came to England in search of the mysterious *marchese* and his granddaughter. She cringed from the knowledge of Nicolò's sheer cold-bloodedness. Nothing, it seemed, would have deterred him from his purpose.

But what of Giuseppe Cabrini's motives in accepting Nicolò's child as his own, as Gina seemed certain he would? To avoid scandal? To advertise to the world that he wasn't impotent? Who knew what lengths vanity would drive a man to? Or was it simply because to acknowledge what had happened would make it impossible to keep his job with Cacciatore Auto Design?

To challenge Nicolò direct would show a concern which would belie the impression she had striven so hard to give, yet hour by hour her position in his household was becoming more untenable. Hateful though it was to admit, the revelation of Nicolò's treachery had only served to numb her love for him on a temporary basis. Like the injection given at a dentist, the relief had been merely temporary. Now, without treatment, the deadening effects were wearing off and the realisation of the truth dawning with painful clarity. She still loved the man she had married, instinctively, against all reason.

If he had only married her for business reasons she would have stayed with him and tried to make a success of their union. Even if his motives had included a desire to mix his blood with that of a Lorenzo to right the wrongs of the past, that she could have borne. Fool that she was, despite the attitude she'd decided to adopt, she might even have suffered the presence of Gina Cabrini in Nicolò's life for a few more weeks, even months, hoping against hope that the relationship would founder in the course of time. But Gina pregnant—no. That was beyond her tolerance.

She had no option but to leave him and return to England, but before she did she would have to take urgent steps to discover more about the circumstances in the past which had left her grandfather open to intimidation. She caught her lower lip between her teeth as she mulled over the problem. Nonno was an old man and it was possible that he had over-reacted to Nicolò's bullying tactics.

The answer she needed came instantly, and it was not one she welcomed. To date all her information had come from Cesare Brunelli. By his own admission he had followed closely the search for the successor to the Castellone title, and his business card was still in her handbag where she had thrust it with angry disdain, some inner caution warning her not to grind it under her heel as she had marched away from the restaurant.

Obnoxious though she found it, she had no alternative but to swallow her pride and ask her tormentor to put her fully in the picture, in the hope that she would find some clue in the past to her present dilemma.

CHAPTER NINE

CATIA would never know how she managed to get through the rest of the evening. Perhaps she'd discovered a remnant of some hereditary spirit of *noblesse oblige* lurking in her soul, she thought with a grim self-deprecatory humour, as a feeling of weariness overtook her when the launch carrying the last guest departed.

Turning from the jetty and re-entering the ballroom, she found her tension subsiding to relief as she discovered there was no sign of Nicolò. Probably he was giving instructions for the clearing-up operation which would take priority in the later hours of that morning, or maybe he was closeted somewhere with Gina, planning their future in relation to her imminent reconciliation with her husband!

A sharp wave of jealousy pierced her heart as, angry at her own reaction as much as at the humiliating betrayal to which she was being subjected, she made her way across the deserted ballroom towards the elegant staircase. At the threshold of the suite she was sharing with Nicolò she paused, her hand rigid on the door-handle. Suppose she was wrong in the assumptions and Nicolò was already in there awaiting her arrival? She was in no mood for a fight or argument—let alone playing the part of complaisant wife should he demand it.

Her jaw clenched in determination, she opened the door, to breathe a sigh of relief as she felt the emptiness of the suite assault her senses. Quickly she went through the motions of undressing, hanging the beautiful dress with the respect it deserved in the wardrobe before taking a quick shower and slipping on the glamorous nightdress which was freshly laundered for her each morning.

Bone-tired with the weariness which came from despair, she laid her golden head on the silk pillow, her last conscious thought that if Nicolò was indeed with Gina she had little to fear when he finally did decide to join her.

It was the bright rays of the morning sun filtering through the Venetian blinds which awakened her. Instantly she knew the bed beside her had never been slept in. So Nicolò had spent the whole night with his beloved—the mother-to-be of his child! A glance at the clock on the bedside table showed her it was eight-thirty. Astonished that she'd enjoyed a good night's rest, and feeling considerably refreshed for the experience, she clambered out of bed, showering and dressing as hastily as possible to suit the climate in a flared cotton skirt in a bold turquoise and orange print topped by a sleeveless turquoise blouse which she knotted beneath her midriff.

The warmth struck her bare arms as she sauntered out on to the terrace where, as had been customary in Nicolò's absence, a table was already laid for her breakfast. Two places had been set, but by the time she'd finished eating the warm rolls and apricot conserve served by an attentive Maria there was still no sign of Nicolò. Expecting the young maid to enquire as to his whereabouts, she was surprised when Maria said nothing. Presumably she, in common with the other servants, had a very good idea where the master of the *palazzo* took his pleasures and was not unduly disturbed by the fact that marriage had not changed his routine!

Luck was favouring her. Determined more than ever to contact Cesare Brunelli, she'd wondered how she could escape the *palazzo* without making Nicolò suspicious. Now that problem no longer existed.

Finishing her second cup of fragrant coffee, she smiled at Maria as the girl asked if she required any further service.

'*Grazie, no, Maria.*' She pushed her chair away from the table, rising to her feet with an inborn grace. 'I think I'll go and spend some of my husband's hard-earned money. My wardrobe could do with an update and Nicolò suggested I do something about it as a priority.'

As the girl nodded her understanding Catia left the terrace. She was in no mood to write notes to her errant husband, but at least if he returned and asked about her whereabouts he would receive an answer, although not one perhaps which he would like!

The suite was still deserted as she pushed open the door and walked towards the gold and onyx telephone. There was no answer from the first number she called but only a few moments after dialling the second she heard the receiver lifted and Brunelli's familiar voice.

'Ah, Marchesa!' There was a note of triumph in his voice as she responded to his brief announcement of his name by giving him her own. 'Have you decided I may be able to assist you after all?'

'I'd like to know more about my own family background,' she said stiffly, hating her own surrender, but powerless to prevent it. 'You did say you'd followed the lawyer's search for my grandfather very closely.'

'And now you find you've got time on your hands and would like to know more about his background?' Catia flinched from the cynicism of his remark, but he continued without pausing. 'Certainly. I'd be delighted to tell you everything I know. I was just leaving for an appointment, and afterwards I intend to spend the day at the Lido. I'll see you in the bar of the Excelsior at eleven—oh, and bring your bikini—they've got their own private beach. *Ciao*!'

The phone went dead before she'd had time to confirm her acceptance of his offer—but then she'd made the request, hadn't she? Still wondering if she'd acted wisely, she grabbed a small informal handbag in which she placed a bottle of sun lotion, some tissues and her purse, treating the journalist's suggestion that she take a bikini with the disdain it merited.

Perhaps the Lido wasn't a bad idea for a rendezvous after all, she decided, her spirits rising as she left the *palazzo* without detection. It would be packed with tourists as well as native Venetians and she could mingle with the crowds unobtrusively without fear of Nicolò pouncing on her from out of nowhere.

Brunelli was waiting for when she arrived. Having taken a *vaporetto* as soon as she'd left the *palazzo*, she'd arrived early after the fifteen-minute trip across the Lagoon and amused herself by watching some energetic tourists playing tennis before making her way to the Excelsior.

'No bikini?' Cesare Brunelli eyed her small handbag with assumed desolation. 'I was looking forward to seeing more of the charms which captivated Nicolò Cacciatore.'

'Really?' she asked coolly. 'I thought it was your theory that my husband's eyes were already occupied elsewhere.' Was he aware of Gina Cabrini's pregnancy? She braced herself for the humiliating details but none came.

'And you're jealous? Who can blame you?' He finished his campari and soda and snapped his fingers at the barman. 'What will you drink, Marchesa?'

'This isn't a social meeting!' The colour rose in her cheeks. 'And if you must address me as anything, it would be better if you called me Catia.'

'I'm honoured, Catia, but I am here at your request and, if we are to do business, then we do it my way: a drink at the bar and afterwards lunch—I already have a table booked.'

'I have to get back to the City...' A mental picture of Nicolò's furious face swam before her eyes.

'Then the sooner we eat, the better!' The Italian took her arm and guided her towards the dining-room. 'I don't know why you are protesting—after all, it won't be the first time I've paid for your meal, will it?'

Holding her tongue, Catia allowed him to lead her to their table, painfully aware that this man could make mischief for Nicolò and his company. That wasn't what she wanted.

It wasn't until they'd finished their meal that Brunelli agreed to answer her questions.

Aghast, she listened to a tale of vendetta and vengeance as the journalist told her the history of the Cacciatore and Lorenzo families, describing in detail the facts he had gleaned as the search for the heir to the old *marchese* had progressed. It was a tale of Italy's deep south, of a quarrel over land between the Cacciatore family who were farmers, and Leopoldo Guido di Castellone, who was the local landowner. It was a story of outrage, cruelty and poverty which horrified her. Nicolò had mentioned the cruelty of her ancestor but hadn't dwelt on his atrocities. Cesare Brunelli seemed to delight in delineating each and every one of his documented sins.

She had already toyed with the idea that Nicolò's motive had been vengeance, if not against her personally, against the memory of the man who had ill-treated his own family. An uneasy shiver traversed her spine as she recalled the harsh, proud face of her husband, the way he had deceived her, and felt sure that Nicolò was a man who would stop at nothing to avenge those he loved.

'You look pale, Catia? Is the sun too much for your English complexion?'

Wearily she shook her head. 'It isn't pleasant having to listen to such a catalogue of sins, as you must know,' she reprimanded him.

'Especially when you wonder about your own husband's motives, eh, Catia?' Brunelli pursed his lips questioningly. 'Barely two weeks after your grandfather had been located, and the fact widely publicised, Nicolò Cacciatore was on his way to England. Ostensibly on business. Strange, then, that he should call in on an old enemy, no? Stranger still that within weeks of meeting his granddaughter, and to the shock of the cognoscenti of Venice, he had proposed marriage to her?' His voice lowered, became confiding. 'How did he manage that, Catia? What pressure did he bring to bear on you and the old man? Or did he simply tell you that he fell in love with you at first sight—and you believed him?'

Her blue eyes widened in her pale face, betraying the truth, and for a moment she thought she saw a glimpse of pity on Brunelli's face.

'So it's just as I supposed.' He regarded her thoughtfully. 'Not only did he deceive the Cabrini woman but you too—and your grandfather...'

Again her expression must have betrayed her, or it was a journalist's instinct which made the Italian frown. 'Your grandfather knew what was happening?'

Too unhappy to consider the wisdom of what she was saying, Catia blurted out unhappily, 'I believe that my...' the word 'husband' jarred in her throat and she abandoned it '... that Nicolò had some means of persuading my grandfather to approve the match. A debt of honour. Something like that. I thought perhaps that you...?' She let the question tail away into silence.

'A debt of honour?' The Italian regarded her, his expression thoughtful. 'Possible, I suppose. As you're aware, Antonio Lorenzo left Italy very quickly after your parents' accident to set up home in England. As far as I know he was never a wealthy man, and the move must have been expensive. There's some evidence that he was acquainted with Paolo Cacciatore—your present father-in-law. Their positions had been somewhat reversed, of course, by then. It was the Cacciatore family who had all the money. Of course Nicolò was only about ten years of age at the time, but the ways of the *faida* are like the mills of God—they grind slowly to achieve their aim. Perhaps Paolo Cacciatore lent Antonio Lorenzo money for the move, knowing he would be unable to repay it, and fully aware that he had a female grandchild who in time could repay the debt with her name.'

'That's horrendous!' Catia protested. But although it was supposition it fitted the facts as she knew them. Oh, dear heavens! Nonno had been desperate to care for her himself when she'd been orphaned and had seen the only way possible to do so was by sharing a house with Aunt Becky. Worse still, he had known he would never be able to repay the debt to his old enemy, so he had changed his name to avoid detection. Suddenly everything was clear: his objection to her learning Italian, his refusal to return to Italy, his apparent dislike of his fellow countrymen. Then a quirk of fate had resulted in his being tracked down...and she had paid off his debt, with her heart, her soul and her body.

'Is that what you wanted to hear?' Brunelli was regarding her curiously.

'It will suffice, yes.' She turned away so he wouldn't see the tears gathering in her eyes, choking in her throat. The two men she had cared for most in the world—and each had betrayed her. Even then, some deep undisturbed remnant of love demanded that she continue to protect Nicolò from the scavengers. 'But it's supposition. Publish it and I'll deny every word!'

'I admire your loyalty. Not many newlywed wives would treat a rival like Gina Cabrini with such equanimity. If you want vengeance now is your time to exact it.'

'There's been too much of that already.' She rose to her feet with dignity, blinking away the last vestiges of water from her eyes. 'For your information, there is nothing between my husband and Gina Cabrini. I know for a fact that the Cabrinis are discussing a reconciliation!'

'I can quote you on that?' Cesare Brunelli's eyes sparkled.

'Why not check it out first and quote Signora Cabrini herself? A "scoop", don't you call it? A far better outcome for you than if you publish the misleading photograph of her with my husband.'

She turned on her heel confident that she'd saved Nicolò's company embarrassment, mocking herself for being unable to uproot the last vestiges of the love which had been seeded and grown in the halcyon days in England.

The *vaporetto* which took her back to the City was packed and she spent the short journey staring unseeingly at the beauty of the lagoon. If her conclusions were correct then she would honour Nonno's debt herself, however great. After all, it was her grandfather's money which had sustained her throughout her training to become a qualified physiotherapist and her skills could be utilised to good effect in repaying him for all his loving care. She bit her lip thoughtfully. Perhaps the answer would be to get a job in a hospital near to Suddingham so that she could live with her grandfather and Aunt Becky. That way she could avoid the astronomical expense of living in London, help Nonno to cope with the day-to-day expenses and at the same time save every spare penny towards repaying the Cacciatore family the debt they were owed. If it took her a lifetime—then so be it!

It wouldn't be easy to face her grandfather, but surely when he knew all the facts he would see how intolerable her position was?

She was still pondering ways and means as she walked through the narrow streets towards the *palazzo*. Despite the image she had tried to portray to alienate him she was certain Nicolò wouldn't let her go voluntarily. She was his 'pound of flesh' and he had already demonstrated how determined he was to enjoy his prize, so she would have to plan her departure carefully. It would mean biding her time, waiting for him to disappear again as he had that morning.

The *palazzo* was quiet in the heat of the late afternoon as she wended her way into the terraced garden, sighing in relief as she saw it was deserted. What she needed now was to cool down in the air-conditioned sanctuary of the apartment and work out her plans in detail.

The Venetian blinds were closed as she entered the dimly lit sitting-room and she expelled her breath with pleasure as the cool air struck her heated skin.

'Was your shopping trip successful, Caterina?'

She gasped as Nicolò's voice made the polite enquiry and his tall figure rose from one of the armchairs.

'Why are you skulking in the dark?' she demanded angrily, shock and apprehension mingling to send the adrenalin surging through her veins at his unexpected materialisation.

'The room only appears dark because you've recently come in from the sun, *cara mia*. When you become accustomed to it you will find it is pleasantly dim. But you didn't answer my question. What designer masterpieces have you purchased to enchant your admirers and to consolidate your position as a leader of fashion, hmm?'

The question was too soft, his voice too carefully controlled, and now that her pupils were adapting to the lack of light she could see from the tense lines each side of Nicolò's beautiful mouth and the cold glitter of his eyes that it concealed an unspoken danger.

'Nothing. I bought nothing,' she confessed, painfully aware of the small handbag clutched in her fingers. 'There was nothing I liked.'

'Then you should have done your shopping in the heart of Venice—rather than on the Lido.'

The comment, spoken in Nicolò's light, still pleasant voice, served only to make the goosepimples rise on her arms, before anger replaced her unreasonable fear. She had done nothing wrong.

'I changed my mind,' she told him boldly. 'Isn't that a woman's prerogative? Besides——' she paused '—how did you know where I'd been? Did you have the audacity to have me followed?'

'Oh, not you, *cara mia*.' He rose to his full height and moved towards her. 'No, I accepted the lie you told Maria, because although I know you to be venal and irresponsible I had not then suspected you of treachery. The object of my interest was your friend Cesare Brunelli. I have had him shadowed since my return from Milan in order to discover his accomplice.'

'Accomplice?' Sheer amazement made Catia's lips part and remain slightly open as her heart seemed to thump painfully in her chest in response to the presence of an almost tangible tension between them. She was frighteningly aware that beneath Nicolò's apparent air of insouciance a deep, dark anger was simmering.

He moved again to stand between her and the door.

'Such innocence, *carissima*! But then your beautiful face shows nothing of the darkness of your spirit, does it? What was he paying you, Catia? What was he offering you that I could not provide?'

Two fast strides and he'd grasped her shoulders in his strong hands, his grip purposeful. 'Or have you decided you can't face the responsibilities that being my wife entails . . . that you can't bring yourself to bear my children with or without the church's blessing? Is that it, Catia? Did Brunelli offer you money without ties? Was the lure of being a wealthy woman in your own right too much to resist? Tell me! What was the price for attempting to ruin my business?'

The last question was accompanied by a stern shake of her shoulders as she stared back uncomprehendingly at his angry face.

'Nicolò, believe me! I have no idea what you're talking about!' Her blue eyes pleaded with the sable darkness of his mesmerising gaze. 'How could I possibly ruin your business—even if I'd wanted to? I know nothing about it!'

'Only what I was indiscreet enough to confide in you that evening after you surrendered your virginity to me,' he said bitterly. 'You charged a high price for what was my undeniable right to take freely. And you had access to my office on the floor above while I was away, and all the time in the world to photograph the projected designs of our new model.' He arraigned her relentlessly. 'The designs which appeared in the newspaper Brunelli serves with such industry.' One hand left her arm to lace through her hair, the fingers tight against her scalp as he forced her head away from him, gazing down into her stricken face, his countenance as cold and hard as if it had been carved by Michelangelo himself. 'How much you must hate me, and how delighted you must have been when I was summoned to Milan to deal with the disaster!'

'I've never been upstairs!' she gasped. 'I wouldn't know where to look. And despite everything that's happened between us I could never betray you like that.'

'Do you know, I almost believe you, *carissima*.' His other hand rose to her face, taking her chin, pinioning it with supple fingers. 'Almost, but not quite. Perhaps if I didn't know what an excellent actress you are, I would.' His mouth smiled but his eyes showed no emotion as he continued to mesmerise her with their icy regard. 'But if you are telling the truth, and your excursion today was nothing other than a desire to play the flirt, then you have reason to be pleased. After the first unauthorised publication of some of our preliminary designs, I deliberately planted false plans in the office here. If Brunelli publishes them or sells them to a rival he will lose all credibility, and you, my dear, will have to face the consequences.'

'He won't—he can't!' Her voice was harsh with anguish. 'At least not through my agency, Nicolò! You must believe me!'

'Must I?' A slow cruel smile transformed his face. 'What other reason would you have to spend so much time in Brunelli's company? Tell me—is he your lover, Catia?'

'Of course not!' She tried to step away but Nicolò was too quick for her, raising a hand to weave it through her hair, pinioning her head with his lean fingers, forcing her to stare up into his angry face. 'He sought me out. He was interested in the way we met . . . how Nonno inherited the title . . .'

'But not in possessing your beautiful body?' He pulled her hard against his own tense frame so that her whole being was filled with his essence, the sweet sun-washed scent of his skin. Strong arms made escape impossible as her soft breasts were crushed against his chest and her thighs met the muscled hardness of his own.

His ragged breathing, the pulsating warmth of his impassioned body, the luminous dark-pupilled eyes, transmitted their own purpose. By denying a conspiracy with Brunelli she had not escaped from the danger which threatened her, just changed its source. He was violently, burningly angry with her. If she had been a man he would have beaten her into submission, but the delicate composition of her female body had changed the goal of his retribution. Desire and anger were fed by the same hormones. The knowledge appalled her.

She opened her mouth to protest her innocence but the words were stillborn as Nicolò lowered his head and kissed her with a near brutal thoroughness which left her gasping.

'I must take part of the blame for neglecting you, *carissima*,' he purred, when, flushed and shaking, he finally released her. 'Brunelli's loss shall be my gain—and what better time to heal our differences than now?'

Despite the inflexion at the end of the sentence it was a statement, not a question.

'Nicolò—no!' Catia tried to disengage herself from his arms but he was too strong for her, holding her with restrained power, while his eyes, bright with sexual desire, dwelt on her troubled countenance.

'Catia—yes!' he mocked. 'Your cold little heart may despise me, but your hot little body is telling me a different story. *Marchesa* or peasant, we may yet find our common ground—in bed.'

His hungry eyes were on her breasts.

'I can't . . .' It was a cry of dissent but it choked in her throat as yet again Nicolò bent his dark head and possessed her mouth with a passionate intensity which drove all kind of protest from her mind.

Automatically she raised her hands to hold his head: to enjoy the feel of his crisp black hair between her fingers. It was madness, but an insanity she could not fight, and the tragedy was that it would always be like this if she stayed with him. He had never loved her, and because she had tried to protect her own vulnerability he now despised her, if not as a traitor, then as an adulteress. Yet physically he found her compatible, and because deep in her heart she had never ceased to love him she was powerless to utter the cry of 'rape' which might have stopped him in his tracks.

His hands dropped to her body, sliding beneath her knotted top, moving against her bare skin with a controlled fervour which made her shudder. Her light bra posed no barrier and a small cry of expectation escaped her lips as Nicolò lowered his head to her exposed breasts.

She was half sobbing with a mounting ecstasy when he raised his head and she felt a tiny surge of triumph when she saw the narrowed brilliance of his eyes, and heard his quickened breathing.

Closing her eyes as he lifted her and carried her through the communicating door to the bedroom, she felt the softness of the bed yield beneath her and Nicolò's hands begin to strip her with unexpected gentleness.

'Look at me, Marchesa.' His voice, dark and beguiling, demanded her attention. 'Look at the man who is your master, whether you like it or not. I want to see your face when I take what is rightly mine.'

'I don't love you, Nicolò!' It was a lie, but, stung by his callousness, it was the only way she could preserve herself from total humiliation.

'But you do desire me, Catia!' He was as naked as she, poised above her, his face subtly altered by the demands of his strong, virile body. 'Why fight your fate? You sold your virginity and your beauty for a palace, but you cannot deny that your body was ripe for a man's possession, or that I am able to please you in bed.'

She couldn't deny it, nor would she try as he coaxed and caressed her to the point where she was pleading for release, begging him to cut her loose from the ties which confined her to the gracious room in the *palazzo*, to set her free as the birds which followed the plough in the Suffolk fields she loved: free as the horses which galloped on Newmarket's luscious grass.

At last he granted her the fulfilment she craved, taking his own pleasure at the same time, so that afterwards they lay exhausted, their bodies entwined, their hearts thundering, sharing the sweet sadness of passion's anticlimax.

It was Nicolò who broke the spell, pulling himself up on one elbow to stare expressionlessly at her spread-eagled form as if he was mentally photographing her physical abandonment.

'So—have I proved my point?'

The coldness of the question was hurtful, and she turned her head away from him to conceal the sudden rise of tears in her eyes.

'Good! Because while you were sunbathing and dining with Brunelli under the pretext of replenishing your wardrobe, I visited the priest to arrange for our nuptials to be celebrated by the church. The ceremony will take place in two weeks' time.'

'How dare you make any such arrangement without consulting me . . . ?' Horror replaced despair as Catia pushed herself upright, her face flushing with anger at his arrogance in ignoring her specific wishes. 'I've already told you——'

'*Silenzio*!' Nicolò's voice was as dark as his thunderous expression. 'Unfaithful, treacherous—whatever your sins, it makes no difference. I chose you as my wife and nothing will alter that. I will not insult my parents by turning my back on their expectations, nor do I intend our children to be ashamed of us! I had hoped you would conform to my wishes, but, since that hope seems optimistic, then the ceremony shall proceed without your agreement.' His eyes burned into the naked body she tried, too late, to hide from his scornful appraisal. 'Whatever our differences, we will always know where to come to settle them! Two weeks, Catia—that's the time you have to come to terms with the situation, if you wish to save your face and your fortune.'

CHAPTER TEN

IT WAS late the following evening before Catia stumbled from the taxi outside her old home at Suddingham, after a nightmare journey across Europe. She'd travelled by train, too distressed to plan a proper itinerary, having to change twice, snatching moments of light sleep when she'd been too exhausted to keep her eyes open, but unable to relax due to the disturbed state of her mind.

Nicolò's remorseless pursuit of his plans had only served to bring forward the strategy already forming in her mind. She had hoped for more time while Nicolò tried to change her mind, but she'd reckoned without his adamantine determination to bind their lives together as strongly as possible.

Not that he would have been able to take her to the Golden Jewel Box by force, but he must have known how hard it would have been for her to defy him once the guests had been invited.

After his stark announcement, Nicolò had left her. Even as he'd showered in the adjoining room she had been planning her escape. Dinner had been a quiet meal taken on the terrace and punctuated only by the minimal courtesies that such an exercise demanded. When Nicolò had told her politely that he intended spending the rest of the evening working she'd jumped at the chance she needed, pleading a headache as an excuse to return to their apartment.

She had waited for an hour in case he should change his mind and then put her plans into action, changing into jeans and a T-shirt topped by her light jacket. All she'd needed was a bag in which to put her money and passport and she could be on her way. At the last moment she'd added her make-up bag and a handful of tissues as well as her hairbrush. Strange how little she needed and how much she was prepared to leave behind.

A shaft of pain had torn through her as her gaze had lingered on the bed she'd shared with so much joy with the man she was about to leave. Despite the way in which he'd made love to her, Nicolò had never cared for her as a person. She'd shivered, ashamed of the way she'd surrendered herself so completely to his meretricious charm.

Glancing down at her left hand, her gaze had been caught by her wedding-ring and the ruby and diamond cluster beneath it. Meaningless symbols of a love that had never existed. Carefully she eased them over her knuckles and placed them on Nicolò's pillow. They would tell him everything he needed to know. Her conscience thus mollified, she'd left the apartment, making her way quietly and unobtrusively down the magnificent staircase.

A few minutes later she'd gained the small door which, after watching some of the earlier preparations for the party, she'd discovered led to the basement. From there a passage led to another door which opened to a flight of stone steps which would take her up to the landing-stage outside the *palazzo*.

Fortunately, there was no sign of Giovanni, but there was a water taxi cruising past, presumably on the offchance of picking up a fare. Thankfully she'd summoned it, glad that Nicolò had been so generous with his cash.

There was no way she was going to be able to board a plane at Marco Polo airport at that time of the night. Her only other option was to go to the railway station and hope to get on a train. Any train, going anywhere, as long as it took her away from Venice and Nicolò Cacciatore. Entering the enclosed cabin, she had sunk down on the comfortable seat, leaning her head back as the boat eased its way out of the minor canal into the mainstream traffic. It was only as the taxi had left the restricted area of the Grand Canal and entered the wider lagoon, picking up speed as it progressed, that her icy calm had melted and she'd begun to weep in earnest.

She'd finally reached Calais more by luck than judgement and had had to wait for the ferry. On reaching Dover it had been necessary to change her remaining handfuls of *lire* and *francs* into sterling before continuing her journey. Since there hadn't been enough left to enable her to hire a car all the way to Suddingham, she'd had to make do with trains and taxis.

Now at last she was home and all she wanted was to throw her weary bones down on her old bed. But first she would have to face her grandfather, make him understand why she'd been unable to keep the bargain he'd made on her behalf.

It was Aunt Becky who came to the door in answer to her summons on the bell.

'Dear heavens!' The older woman's face drained of colour. 'Catia, darling, what on earth's happened? Why are you here?' She stood back, allowing her niece to enter, enfolding her in her arms as soon as she was over the threshold. 'Oh, darling, what is it?'

'I've left Nicolò.' Too tired to break the news gently, Catia blurted out the truth. 'He doesn't love me. He never did!'

Somewhere a door opened and Catia lifted her face from the comfort of her aunt's shoulders as she heard her grandfather's querulous voice.

'Catia? *Santo cielo*! Why didn't you let us know that you were coming? And where's Nicolò?'

'Because I didn't have time to tell you, Nonno.' Moving from Becky's embrace, she went to her grandfather, holding out her hands in unconscious appeal. 'And Nicolò's still in Venice. I've left him, Nonno. Our marriage is over. I want a divorce.'

'Divorce! *Sciocchezza*! The Lorenzos do not recognise such an abomination. So you've had a fight?' He shrugged his shoulders, his expression stern. 'That is nothing new among newlywed couples. But to run away? That's an irresponsible action, but one which I'm sure your husband will forgive when you return to him if you are truly penitent.'

Despite her weariness, anger flared in Catia's heart. 'It's not I who should be penitent! Nicolò's behaviour has been unforgivable, and I've no intention of going back to him—ever!'

Antonio Laurence's face remained stern. 'Nicolò is a man, with a man's strengths and desires. He has no need to account to his wife for his actions.'

Surely she couldn't be hearing this? But her grandfather's face betrayed no sign of understanding or mercy. Of course, he was of a different generation, steeped in the old mores and customs of his old homeland, but to pass judgement without any evidence . . . !

'Even if those actions include beating me?' Her conscience twinged slightly, but she comforted herself that she'd not actually accused Nicolò of that crime. It was merely a supposition to bring her grandfather to face up to his arbitrary ruling.

'If that was the case then you must have deserved it,' came the remorseless reply which left her gasping.

'Antonio, please, the child is on her last legs. Surely you must see that? What she needs now is food and sleep. Tomorrow she'll see things differently.' Becky came to her rescue, her voice quiet and soothing.

'Let's hope so.' Antonio Laurence's face softened as he held out his arms to his granddaughter. 'Becky is right. You do look exhausted. Believe me, a good night's rest and in the morning you'll realise how silly you've been.'

'No!' Defiantly she faced him, knowing the time of reckoning had come. 'It's no good, Nonno. I've found out the truth. Nicolò never loved me. It was all a sham. All he ever wanted was to marry into the house of Castellone. When he discovered you had inherited the title of *marchese*, he sought me out deliberately because I was your granddaughter!' Her voice broke on a sob of emotion. 'Everything he said to me was a lie! He was already in love with another woman in Milan.'

She paused for breath, raising a hand to the wall to support herself as her legs seemed about to let her down. 'But you, Nonno,' she asked painfully into the ensuing silence. 'Why didn't you tell me the truth about your past? The hold that Nicolò had over you? Why did you let me find out the hard way that the marriage had been arranged between the two of you?'

'The title was an anachronism. I couldn't reject it but I could ignore it,' Antonio Laurence said gruffly, avoiding her gaze.

'But Nicolò couldn't, could he?' Her eyes reflected the pain that seared her heart. 'If it hadn't been for the title, he would never have come to England or sought me out, or deceived me into marrying him. He would never have known of my existence. And he would never have demanded you repay an outstanding debt by allowing me to walk blindly into such a dreadful liaison.'

She paused for a second, her soft heart touched by the pallidity of her grandfather's face, then continued steadily, 'Please don't deny it, Nonno, I overheard the two of you talking after the reception——'

'*Non è vero!*' Antonio Laurence's dark eyes blazed with a sudden anger as he interrupted, dismissing her claim. 'Oh, I don't deny the marriage was arranged, but not in the way you assume. It was I who arranged it, not Nicolò. It was for your sake—your protection. Yes, there was a debt of honour involved, but it was Paolo Cacciatore—Nicolò's father—who was the debtor, not I. Nicolò Cacciatore met and wooed and married you because *I* asked him to. No...' He paused as Catia's jaw dropped in horrified astonishment. 'Not asked, but demanded! It was I who called in the debt, Catia—and Nicolò who paid it.'

The sleeping-tablets Becky had insisted on her taking had served their purpose. It was eight in the morning when Catia awakened after twelve hours of dreamless sleep.

Her mind still befuddled, she could only vaguely recall her reaction to her grandfather's stark statement the previous evening: the sudden narrowing of her vision as darkness had begun to close around her. It had been Aunt Becky who had taken control, guiding her tired body to a chair, insisting that she have a cup of coffee and plying her with a selection of food, which reluctantly she'd eaten because it seemed the easiest option at the time.

As for her grandfather...with a surprising show of iron will Becky had insisted on his leaving the two women together. Desperate to get him to elaborate on his bald statement, Catia nevertheless had lacked the strength, physical or mental, to insist on a full explanation.

When her aunt had handed her the sleeping-tablets she'd demurred, but Becky had been insistent, and in retrospect she'd been right. Catia had to admit that she did feel physically rested, although her mind and her emotions seemed unusually numb.

Having been too exhausted the previous evening to do anything other than to fall into bed, she started the day with a warm, leisurely bath before raiding her wardrobe for something suitable to wear among the garments she had previously decided to discard. Black jeans and a long-sleeved pale blue cotton sweater seemed suitable for the mild but damp June day and an old pair of scuffed trainers provided a comfortable covering for her feet.

Brushing her hair, she caught it back at her neck with a length of black ribbon before carefully applying a light make-up to her face. Frankly she had no interest in her appearance, with the weight of sorrow which was dragging her down, but it was a symbolic action. She would have to assume a brave face in order to accept whatever explanation Nonno was prepared to give her, and this would be a start in the right direction.

Whatever his motives for organising such an appalling travesty, she knew deep down that Antonio Laurence loved her. She would listen calmly to his explanation and then, and only then, would she judge him for the way he had ruined her life. But, whatever the outcome, her worst fears had already been confirmed. Nicolò had never loved or wanted her, although at times the act he had put on had been very convincing. Ruthlessly she clamped her jaw and swallowed hard, determined not to let the threatening tears fall. She'd been used as a pawn by two of the people she loved most in the world—something to be played to gain an advantage before being made expendable.

The circumstances might have changed—but the result was the same. Nicolò had never loved her, never wanted her as his wife. She felt sick with humiliation. It was Nicolò who had been wronged by having an unwanted wife foisted on him, yet he'd been prepared to honour the agreement, even in the face of her own mulishness. Dear God! How he must have hated her when she'd started to play the part of the shrew...

Aunt Becky was already in the kitchen when she entered it, attracted by the smell of bacon and eggs.

'I heard you running your bath, so I started on your breakfast.' Becky dished out a large helping, adding a slice of fried bread and a sausage. 'Here you are, love. We might as well eat in the kitchen as there's only the two of us.'

Perched on one of the kitchen stools, Catia's mouth began watering at the delicious aroma of the plate before her, and unexpectedly she discovered she was ravenously hungry.

'Two of us?' she queried. 'Where's Nonno, then?'

'Still in bed.' Becky poured out two cups of coffee and handed one over as she took her own place at the breakfast bar. 'He tends to lie in longer these days and I don't disturb him. He'll ask for his breakfast when he's ready, but yesterday's events upset him, I'm afraid, and he may not put in an appearance till nearer lunchtime.'

'They upset me too,' Catia pointed out drily. 'The one thing I never even considered was that my grandfather would feel it was his duty to buy me a husband. It was bad enough when I thought he'd been forced into agreeing to a marriage—but to find out that he had instigated it...' She shook her blonde head in despair.

Becky regarded her sadly. 'I heard what Antonio said to you, but I know nothing more. It came as a shock to me too—I really thought you and Nicolò were hopelessly in love with each other.'

'Yes, so did I.'

Catia finished her breakfast in an uneasy silence, conscious of her aunt's discomfiture. But what had occurred wasn't Becky's fault. She and Nonno had lived together amicably, their sole purpose in life to provide a loving home for her, Catia, but that was all. Both had kept their own counsel, their own secrets.

So she would have the morning to kill before she could even begin to get to the bottom of the plot her grandfather had devised and the reason behind it. Normally she could exercise patience. In her work at the hospital it had been a necessity, but how could she occupy herself until Nonno chose to put in an appearance? The answer came to her in a flash. She would walk over to the Carvilles' place and see if she could cadge a ride. It was the one thing which she knew she would enjoy despite the cloud of depression which encompassed her.

Richard welcomed her with a grin of delight as she walked into the exercise yard.

'Catia! How marvellous to see you. Don't tell me your husband wants to buy another horse?'

'No.' Forcing a smile to her lips, she shook her head. 'I wondered if there was a chance of a ride.'

'Sure.' He cast her a speculative look. 'Nicolò not with you?'

'No. Not this time.' It sounded terse, but she was in no mood to explain herself, even to Richard.

'Right. I'll ask one of the lads to saddle up Treasure for you. Here you are, you'd better wear this.' He cast a critical eye over her garb as he handed her a hard riding hat. 'And take it easy. Treasure's not used to a hard gallop.'

It was good advice and Catia followed it, content to mix walking with cantering as she followed a bridle path through the woods towards the open fields.

It was nearly eleven o'clock when she returned to the stables, and the yard appeared deserted as she walked the mare towards her box. But as she swung her leg over the saddle she heard the sound of a man's footsteps approaching somewhere behind her.

'We had a marvellous ride!' she called out brightly, patting the mare's neck and being rewarded by a whinny of pleasure.

'I'm delighted to hear it, *cara*.'

Not Richard but Nicolò! Dressed from neck to ankle in black: black jeans, black cotton roll-neck sweater, black hair and black eyes which regarded her with a fierceness which belied his pleasant greeting. Morose, masculine and magnificent, he glowered down at her.

'You!' Fear and anger melded to bring a scarlet flush to her cheeks. 'What are you doing here? How did you find me?'

'I'm here to take you back to Venice with me, what else? We have a very important engagement to keep, if you remember. And as for finding you—where else would you run to? After I'd satisfied myself that Brunelli wasn't offering you a bed for the night, it was just a matter of waiting for your grandfather to phone me and confirm your arrival—which he did last night.'

'You didn't lose much time in coming,' she remarked bitterly, recalling her own tortuous journey.

'Fortunately the company jet was available. I left Italy in the early hours of this morning and intend to be back in Venice by tonight.'

'Don't let me keep you, then.' With fingers that trembled, she loosed the strap of her riding hat, removing it from her head. Somehow she must also have undone the ribbon which bound her hair, because it swirled in a golden cloud round her shoulders.

'I don't intend to,' he riposted. 'Since you will be returning with me.'

'No.' She shook her head, summoning all her courage. 'Nonno's told me everything. How he entered into a conspiracy with you, how he begged you to take me off his hands as if I were a liability——'

'Not everything, *carissima*.' Two steps and he'd grabbed hold of her, pulling her away from the horse and pinioning her in his arms. 'I've just come from having a long talk with him.'

'Treasure.' Wildly she fought to be free. 'Treasure has to be seen to!'

'So do you, *sposa mia*.' His look was remorseless. 'Treasure knows where her home is, which is more than you seem to.'

As if to confirm his words, the mare trotted quietly towards her box as one of the grooms came forward to remove her tack.

'It's no good, Nicolò.' She drummed angry fists against his adamantine chest, poignantly, bitterly re-calling how similar the circumstances were to those when she'd first realised how desperately she loved him. 'I don't know what your motives were in obliging my grandfather and I no longer care. Go back to Gina and acknowledge your child. If she loves you as much as you love her she'll leave her husband for you. I intend to sue you for divorce in the English courts on the grounds of unreasonable behaviour—hopefully I won't have to wait the statutory two years when I produce all the evidence, and you can marry your mistress and give a proper name to your offspring!'

'*Dio*! Is there no stopping your tongue?'

'After what you and my grandfather have done to me?' She made a half-hearted attempt to free herself by jabbing at one of his legs with one of her trainers. 'You'd have to cut it out with a knife to make me silent.'

'Ah, *tesoro mio*.' He dealt her a grim smile, neatly sidestepping her cushioned sole. 'Believe me, what I've done to you to date is nothing to what I am going to do to you in the near future if you don't quieten down and give me a hearing.'

'You——' she began heatedly, but the words died in her throat as he drew her hard against his chest, lowering his head to possess her angry mouth, kissing her with an impassioned fire that had her gasping for breath when he finally released her.

'*Selvaggio*!' She spat the insult out, raising her hands to touch her pulsating mouth as Nicolò loosened his hold on her. If the truth be told, he hadn't hurt her as much as he had aroused her. And the latter was by far the worse crime as far as she was concerned when all she wanted to do was to see the back of him—forever!

'A savage, am I, *mia piccola* Caterina?' His eyes glistened with a dark threat beneath the thick brush of lashes.

'Yes—no—yes!' She had lain in his arms, welcomed him into her body, experienced his gentleness as well as his passion, but now her heart beat faster, fuelled by the adrenalin of fear.

'Then you do well to be afraid of me, *moglie mia*, because a savage wouldn't think twice about beating a disobedient and faithless wife, before dragging her back to his bed.'

'I've n-never been unfaithful to you, Nicolò,' she stuttered, horrified that his remark held such an accusation. 'You're not really suggesting that because Cesare Brunelli paid for my lunch or because I met him on the Lido it meant there was anything like that between us?'

'No.' His smile was strangely gentle. 'I didn't ever believe that, but despite his profession Brunelli does seem to possess a maverick charm for women, and you'd made it very clear to me that you didn't love me. I wasn't inclined to take chances.'

'I found him totally distasteful,' Catia said coldly.

'Indeed,' Nicolò concurred. 'I was delighted to be able to wring the same admission from him—as well as a very comprehensive account of what he'd been up to.'

'Did you hurt him?' Wide-eyed, she stared at his taciturn face.

Nicolò shrugged. 'Only his pride—personal and professional. And, now he understands exactly how matters rest, the time has come to put you fully in the picture too. Come!' He grasped her firmly by her upper arm and began to lead her across the yard.

'Where are you taking me?' There was a grimness in his expression, a certain set to his jaw that betokened her ill.

'You want to discuss our private affairs here in front of the stable staff?'

Catia shot a quick glance towards where the groom was seemingly intent on rubbing down Treasure's thick coat. 'Not particularly... but——'

'Richard has kindly lent us the use of the tack-room so we can sort out our differences in peace.'

She went with him because she had little option. She was seeing the steel behind the velvet, and instinct told her that if she didn't go with him voluntarily he would sweep her up into his arms and take her there anyway. Better to retain her dignity in the face of such adamantine resolve.

'Splendid! This will suit our purpose nicely, I think.' Ushering her in, he turned to close the door behind them. The room was small and warm, smelling of saddle-soap, leather and polish. A few bridles and bits and other pieces of equine accoutrement were neatly hung on nails driven into the wall, while what were obviously Richard's riding boots were standing on a low shelf, glowing with loving care.

'Sit down, Catia.' Nicolò's dark head nodded towards the only chair in the room as he himself perched one lean, muscular hip on the tack table. Silently she obeyed him. Golden-tongued he might be, but he would never be able to persuade her that he had ever cared one atom for her!

'Well?' she encouraged him, tilting her head, meeting his dark gaze with fearless blue eyes. 'You can start by telling me why my grandfather begged you to marry me—and why you accommodated him.'

'Protection.' The one word hung in the air between them as Catia shook her head uncomprehendingly. 'Protection,' Nicolò repeated. 'Your protection, Catia.' He paused, his gaze lingering on her startled face, before speaking again. 'Brunelli admitted that he has already told you about the *faida* between our two families in the past, so I won't bore you by repeating the history. Enough to say that the law of the *faida* is that all members of the family involved must be exterminated to cleanse the honour of the offended family.'

'But that's barbarous!' Catia protested. 'What are you telling me, Nicolò? That grandfather brought me to England because—oh!' Her hands rose to her throat as if she were protecting it from some predator. 'My parents—are you saying that it was a Cacciatore who killed my parents?'

'No! No, I'm not!' He was on his feet, standing over her, his fists clamped hard against his sides. 'Your parents were killed in an accident. An accident, Catia, I swear it. As the children of both sides grew older, became more educated and moved away from the region, the *faida* had ceased to be actively pursued. Gradually the two family names began to die out—Lorenzo because of lack of progeny and Cacciatore because of the predominance of female children. But your grandfather never forgot the past.'

'But Nonno believed my father and mother had been victims of a murder?' A deep sense of sadness invaded her spirit as a surge of insight illuminated her mind.

'Yes.' Nicolò swallowed convulsively. 'Apparently he was distraught. He made his views known at the time and a very thorough investigation was carried out. There was never any doubt but that the tragedy was a freak accident.'

'But my grandfather couldn't accept that?'

Nicolò sighed. 'He was, I think, a little mad at the time. His one thought was to protect you. So he brought you back to England to your mother's country and to your mother's aunt, because he knew and trusted her.'

'Poor Nonno.' Emotion blocked Catia's throat. 'How he must have suffered. But I still don't understand. If he thought your family had been responsible for his son's death, why would he want to hand me over to——?' She looked away, unable to meet his eyes as she perceived the torment in them.

'To me?' Bitterly he completed the sentence for her. 'Catia, you remember the first time you ran away from me in Venice—and I found you at that café with some English boy?'

How would she ever forget? Silently she nodded her golden head.

'Brunelli had told you something about the past and you taunted me with it?'

'I remember.' She bit her lip. If she'd had the slightest idea of the real facts she would have held her tongue.

'Do you also remember that I told you the old *marchese* had set the dogs on my father and that he would have had his throat torn out if it hadn't been for a friend?'

She shuddered. 'I've never forgotten it.'

'That friend was your grandfather. Paolo, my father, was twelve years old at the time and Antonio Lorenzo was six years his senior. It appears that your grandfather was a very distant Lorenzo cousin and was there on sufferance for some family funeral. When the *marchese* gave the order for the dogs to be released, he was horrified at such barbarity, and rushed out to try to prevent it. He was too late for that, but he did manage to put the dogs off the scent by acting as the quarry, so my father could escape unharmed.'

'He was very brave!' At least she had one ancestor of whom she could be proud.

'Indeed he was, because although he outran the dogs there was no way he could outrun the thrashing the *marchese* ordered for him as his reward for interfering. Such gossip passes quickly through small villages, and when my father told his own parents how Antonio had saved him they made a point of tracing him when he returned to his own home in Naples, to thank him.

'At the time they were very poor and a reward was beyond them—not that Antonio expected or wanted one—but my father swore that he would be in Antonio's debt all his life and that your grandfather only had to call on him should he ever need help.' He smiled bleakly.

'Ironically it was still the rule of the *faida* which was operating, but this time for good. Do you understand?'

He held her blue gaze, his jaw taut, a small muscle at the corner of his mouth betraying some tightly held emotion as he waited for her reply.

Her lips parted slightly from the shock of realisation, but she met his unwavering stare with simple dignity.

'Yes, I think I do. You mean a life saved for a life saved,' she accorded softly.

CHAPTER ELEVEN

'RIGHT.' Nicolò moved away, thrusting his hands into the back pockets of his jeans, hunching his broad shoulders as he began to pace the floor. 'Time passed. My father was intelligent and he worked hard. Turning his back on the land, he got a job as a waiter and saved hard until he was able to start his own snack bar. When he was twenty-five he married happily, but his first wife died after twenty years of marriage without ever bearing him a child.

'After a period of mourning he met and married his present wife, Rosa, a lady who is nineteen years his junior and my mother.'

'While Antonio—my grandfather——'

'Married Sara, who tragically died giving birth to your father—Alessandro.'

'My father was thirty-seven when he died and my mother just two years younger.' It was impossible to stop the tears which rolled effortlessly down her cheeks. 'I can't even remember them.'

'You were two years old.' Nicolò stopped pacing, his handsome face drawn and angry. 'But I swear it was an accident. An act of God, if you like. My family were innocent but, as I've told you, nothing would persuade your grandfather of the truth at the time. His one thought was to preserve you from the *faida*. Your own mother had been an orphan but Antonio had met her aunt, Rebecca, when Alessandro had been courting her, and with Rebecca's co-operation he brought you to England, anglicised your name to Laurence, and there the matter would have ended if he hadn't inherited the title of Marchese di Castellone. Oh, the old *marchese* who had beaten him had long since died and the title had passed further and further from the source, until only Antonio was left.'

Slowly Catia shook her head. 'I remember him going through a period of depression at the beginning of the year, but I thought he must be ill or have money worries.'

'No, he'd received the letter from the lawyers in Italy and he'd also learned that the search for the owner of the title had caught the imagination of the public. His sanctuary had been invaded. As he saw it, only you and he remained from the original Lorenzo line, and he was an old man. Death would probably claim him before the *faida*—but you... You, Catia, were young and beautiful, dearly loved, and totally oblivious of the danger which lurked round every corner!'

'But you said the *faida* had died out!'

'Oh, my darling, it has.' He came towards her and took her hands, enfolding them in his own, bending his head to kiss their chill surface. 'But your grandfather was living in the past. To him it was still alive, still threatening those whom he loved the most. It was then he decided to call in the debt Paolo Cacciatore had acknowledged he owed.

'My father's chain of snack bars is well established, although he no longer takes an active part in running them, but it was easy enough for Antonio to obtain his private address. In fact I believe he used the same firm of lawyers who had originally traced him to England.'

'I'm not sure I understand,' Catia said in a small voice, although already she was beginning to see how her grandfather's mind had worked.

'It's quite simple really. Of all the Cacciatore family, your grandfather knew that Paolo, my father, could be trusted implicitly. He wrote to him begging his patronage, imploring him to use whatever influence he had over the rest of the family to ensure your life was never put in danger. But my father had a better idea. He knew you were in no danger but he saw the opportunity to reunite the families of himself and the man who had saved his life, to put an end to Antonio's fears so that he could live his remaining years in peace.'

It took some courage to say it, but courage was something Catia had never lacked, and she needed to hear the admission from Nicolò's own lips, although the words would lacerate her heart. 'Your father asked you to redeem his debt of honour, didn't he, Nicolò?' she asked, a sense of total hopelessness overwhelming her. 'He commanded you to make me your wife?'

'Yes.' Releasing her hands, Nicolò returned to his former perch on the table, his voice deep and purposeful as he continued. 'He commanded me to redeem what he saw as a debt of honour, but I refused. Not because I took any pleasure in disobeying him, or because I wished to choose my own wife, although that naturally was a consideration, but because it would have done you a great disservice, to pretend an emotion which I didn't feel. And that was what I should have had to do if I'd agreed to the plan, since your grandfather was adamant that you should never know of the danger he supposed lay in wait for you.'

'So what changed your mind?' Unable to watch his face, Catia stared down at her clasped hands still bearing the invisible imprint of Nicolò's warm mouth. 'What bribe made the deal irresistible after all? Did your father threaten to disinherit you if you refused?'

'That's not worthy of you, Catia.' A dark flush stained his arrogant face. 'I'm not dependent on my father's fortune, as well you know.'

'But there must have been a reason.' She stared defiantly into his lean, angry face.

'There was. I fell in love with you.'

'But——' Her objection faded as he motioned her to silence.

'My father wrote to Antonio, reassuring him that he no longer had need to fear his old enemies, but he felt that might not be enough, so he asked me to visit your grandfather when I was over here on business. It seemed the least I could do, but what I didn't know was that my father had broached the possibility of marriage between our two families in his letter.' He paused with a sigh. 'It was then that Antonio repeated my father's plea that I should take you under my protection. He insisted on showing me photographs of you, telling me where you lived and where you worked, begging me just to meet you, to get to know you. He was so certain that I'd be unable to resist your charm and your beauty.'

'Oh, how could he?' Catia buried her face in her hands, humiliated beyond belief.

'Because he loved you, *carissima*,' Nicolò responded softly. 'And of course he was right. I left Suddingham, and returned to London haunted by the photographs I'd seen. Was it possible that someone so outwardly beautiful should possess the inner beauty that the photographs seemed to project, and that your grandfather insisted you did? He'd even sworn that the photographs hadn't approached doing you justice.

'I was intrigued and, since I was due to take a holiday, I paid a visit to the hospital where you worked, quite unknown to your grandfather.' He smiled as she raised her face to stare at him with haunted eyes. 'I'd imagined I would have to make several enquiries, but fate was working on my side even then, because I'd hardly been there five minutes when you walked into the outpatients' department with your arm around an elderly woman. Even with your hair secured on the top of your head, and wearing a uniform, there was no mistaking you. And Antonio had been right. Your photographs came nowhere near doing you justice.

'Oh, it wasn't just your physical appearance, although God knows that was reason enough; it was the way you were looking at your patient, the compassion in every line of your body. You were *simpatica*, and every fibre of my body recognised it and hungered to possess you. That was the moment I knew that I loved you, just as Dante knew he loved Beatrice at first sight, as Petrarch knew he loved Laura, and that I would go to any lengths to make you my wife.'

A faint hope stirred in Catia's heart as she met his dark-eyed gaze, but she'd been hurt too much to trust him again so soon, although her love for him lay deep and eternal in her soul; and there were other events he would have to explain—his association with Gina Cabrini, for one—before she would be able to accept the miracle of his assurance, to live with him again as his wife.

He smiled. A brief, wry twist of his strong mouth. 'You can imagine Antonio's delight when I told him I'd reconsidered my decision.'

'He certainly looked much happier when I went back home,' she observed, remembering the way he'd greeted her, the new lightness in his step.

'Of course.' Nicolò shrugged broad shoulders. 'All his worries about your future safety, whether justified or not, were over. He was convinced that you would fall in love with me, and that, after years of voluntary exile, with the two families reunited in friendship by marriage, he could safely return to Italy, the land of his birth; the land he still loved.'

'And then I ran away from you and his dreams were demolished.' Bleakly Catia acknowledged the trauma her action had caused her grandfather.

'Neither of us realised you'd overheard our conversation—and drawn the wrong conclusions.' He gave a bleak laugh. 'But if you were hurt and angry, can you imagine how I felt when your personality seemed to change the moment you set foot in Italy? Why didn't you confide your fears in me, *carissima*?'

Scarlet stained Catia's cheeks. 'I felt used and cheated. It was the only way I could think of to cope with the shattering blow my pride had taken. And I was frightened, Nicolò...' Her eyes beseeched his understanding. 'I didn't know why you had pretended to love me, and I was too proud to ask. The only thing I could think of doing was to distance myself from you while I tried to find out the real reason you'd married me.'

'It was no pretence, *amore mio*. I loved you then as I love you now. Oh, I don't deny I was hurt and angered by your attitude in Venice, confused as well, but I still loved you. *Dio* have you any idea how terrified I was myself when I awakened that first morning and found an empty bed beside me?'

'You were a little angry when I returned,' Catia acknowledged, allowing herself the luxury of a small reminiscent smile, as a dawning happiness spread through every fibre of her body.

'Because for one mad moment I'd even wondered if your grandfather's nightmare of a continuing *faida* wasn't a figment of his imagination after all, and that one of my less noble relatives had made off with you!' He exhaled his breath in a deep sigh. 'If only I'd known what was going on in your head I could have put your mind at rest, but I'd no idea how many seeds of doubt Brunelli had already planted in your imagination. I told myself that it was natural you should want beautiful clothes and jewels to complement your own beauty and that your reluctance to admit you loved me was some kind of game, because in Suddingham I'd had no doubt.' He grimaced. 'I persuaded myself that after we'd become lovers everything would be as I'd hoped and planned—but obviously I overestimated the power of my own performance!'

'Oh, Nicolò, no!' She was on her feet, moving swiftly to stand in front of him, reaching out to touch his face, to wipe the bitterness from his twisted mouth. 'I wanted to love you—I *did* love you—but...' Her voice trailed away to silence.

'You didn't trust me,' he said flatly. 'How can I blame you for that, when I was so blind to your pain, so concerned with my own disenchantment that I neglected you?'

It was the moment above all that Catia had been dreading. She wanted so desperately to believe Nicolò's avowal of love, but how could she when the spectre of Gina still loomed so large between them? She failed to suppress the shudder which undermined her slender frame as she moved away from him, walking towards the window overlooking the yard and staring out into the distance. How could she ever accept his relationship with Gina?

From behind her Nicolò's voice spoke quietly, almost conversationally. 'When I discovered late Saturday night that you'd left me—apparently for good since you'd discarded your rings—I was distraught. I was convinced that Brunelli had been poisoning your mind against me, so I confronted him.' His voice deepened with satisfaction. 'He was very forthcoming, after a little persuasion. Even showed me the photograph of myself and Gina with which he'd taunted you.'

At the window, Catia's shoulders stiffened but still she refused to face him. 'So?'

'So I returned to the *palazzo*, because if you hadn't run to Brunelli the odds were on your making for Suddingham. I phoned Giuseppe Cabrini at his home to tell him I'd be out of Italy for a day or so and Gina answered the phone. She told me the two of you had been talking in the garden and that you'd appeared to know all about her pregnancy and how I'd stood by her.'

Catia cleared her throat in an attempt to keep her voice impersonal. 'She mentioned it and I didn't want to embarrass either of us by declaring my total ignorance.'

'Catia!' She was seized from behind and roughly turned, so that she fell against Nicolò's hard body. 'How could you possibly believe that Gina was carrying my child?' He shook her, not roughly, but enough to encourage her hair to fan against her shoulders. 'You absurd little fool!'

'You mean she's not?' she asked tremulously, a strange wild hope flaring inside her.

Nicolò said something harsh and pithy in Italian which even her extensive vocabulary didn't include. 'Gina has only ever been a friend. We knew each other as children. I introduced her to Giuseppe Cabrini. I was even best man at their wedding!'

'But she said...' Catia's protest died on her lips. What exactly had Gina said? The other woman's exact words escaped her memory.

'Not that I was the father of her child; I'd stake the *palazzo* on that!' Nicolò returned grimly. 'I had no intention of seeing her when I was in Milan, but I wanted to buy you something beautiful to wear for the fashion show, and she was the obvious person to help.' His hands locked hard on her shoulders as he stared down into her tearful eyes. 'I was surprised when she said she wanted to see me, but she was a friend, so I made the time to take her to dinner. She'd walked out on Giuseppe six months ago because of his jealousy and his belief that she was deliberately avoiding having a family so she could pursue her career. Ironically, it was only a few weeks later that she discovered she was carrying his child.'

'Giuseppe's child?' Catia blinked as a rising spiral of hope began to lick through every cell in her body. 'Oh, heavens, I hadn't realised—oh, poor Gina.'

'Exactly,' Nicolò agreed grimly. 'She was still hurt and blazingly angry at the harsh words they'd exchanged and she had determined to keep her pregnancy a secret; to take time off work for the birth and afterwards to bring the child up by herself.

'But as the time elapsed she began to have doubts. Realising deep down that she still loved and missed Giuseppe, she knew she'd never have the heart to keep him from knowing his child.' Nicolò paused, raising his hand to caress Catia's hair with an agonising tenderness. 'But she was afraid, *amore mio*, terrified that he would reject both her and the child because she had waited so long to tell him.'

He inhaled a deep breath, then continued evenly, 'I escorted her back to her apartment and we discussed the best thing to do, and eventually I agreed that I should act as go-between. You see, Giuseppe's both a trusted friend and a colleague of mine, and I know how much he's been missing Gina, although he tries to hide it. If anyone could bring them happily together again it would be me.'

'And I thought that you and she...' Catia whispered hoarsely, ashamed at the way she had misinterpreted Gina's words as joy surged into her heart. 'Oh, Nicolò! Can you ever forgive me?'

'It was my fault from the beginning,' he told her generously, hugging her pliant form to his own. 'I should have followed Gina's advice when she told me to share her secret with you because you were my wife and I should have no secrets from you, but I was angry with your indifference to me and not in the mood to explain myself.'

He laced his fingers through her hair, drawing her head backwards so that she was forced to endure the blazing intensity of his dark gaze. 'Yes, I can forgive you, *carissima*, if you can forgive me; but if you ever run away from me again I'll give you the beating your grandfather believes you've already suffered at my hands!'

He glared ferociously at her, but she smiled at his threat, aware of his inner pain and knowing he would never touch her in anger.

'*Madre di Dio*! Have you any idea of the torture I went through waiting for your grandfather to telephone me and tell me you had arrived at his house? I didn't sleep, wondering whether I'd made the correct decision or if I should report your disappearance to the police and have the canals dragged. Only the knowledge that you were too tender-hearted to bring grief to Antonio and Becky kept me sane, until I received their phone call.'

'And you, Nicolò. I never wanted to hurt you.' She drew in a deep breath, sensing what he wanted to know and exulting in being able to tell him. 'Because I love you. From the first moment I saw you, you brought something special into my life. You made me feel sensations and emotions I'd never known existed. But everything seemed to happen so quickly; it was exciting but it was frightening too, and I was terrified to get too involved with you because I believed Nonno would never agree; instead...' She began to laugh, the tension draining out of her as she held on to Nicolò's shoulders to support her weakening legs. 'Instead, all the time he was acting as a marriage broker...'

Imprisoning her laughing mouth, his kiss ravishingly sweet and insistent, Nicolò caressed the warm curves of her body as she strained against him, craving the imprint of his masculine form against her yielding flesh. Before she realised what was happening he had swung her round so that her back was against the table and he was cushioning her head in his hands as she fell against it, his body hot and demanding on her own.

The pleasure was so intense that she felt no discomfort as she reached to wind her fingers through his thick black hair, drawing his mouth towards her own, whimpering with pleasure as the tip of his tongue traced the sensitive outline of her parted lips.

Her heart was racing, the subtle scent of his body intoxicating her as she moved her round breasts tantalisingly against his hard chest. All her fears and expectations mingled as she yielded to Nicolò's overpowering domination, dissolving into abandoned acquiescence against his hard male contours.

He forsook her mouth to whisper huskily against her cheek, 'I've never felt for any woman the way I feel for you, or been so heartsick as when I thought you'd only married me so you could live in the style you thought you deserved. The first thing I did on arriving in Milan was to have the portrait of you that I'd commissioned in the *piazza* framed and hung in my office to sustain me as I laboured, but it was a poor substitute for the living beauty I'd been forced to leave behind in Venice.' His teeth nipped gently on her earlobe. 'Do you promise never to leave me again?'

'I promise,' she sighed. 'On one condition—that you never again accuse me of stealing your plans and selling them to the Press.'

'Ah, that was wishful thinking, *carissima*. I was angry and confused and I wanted to believe anything except that you found Brunelli more attractive than me.'

'As if I ever could!' Her radiant smile lightened her face. 'But have you found out who was guilty?'

Nicolò nodded. 'Brunelli decided to tell me.' The sparkle in his dark eyes suggested that he had used some persuasion to encourage the admission. 'It was one of the junior draughtsmen who felt himself undervalued. That gentleman has now left the company to find more compatible employment in another industry. He won't trouble us again.'

'You're not prosecuting?'

'No. Our own security was lax and the payment Brunelli made to him has now been voluntarily paid into a charity. Besides, the damage done is not too great. The plans were merely preliminaries and thankfully didn't include our more sophisticated ideas. As far as I'm concerned the matter is closed. I have much more important matters to attend to.'

'Such as?' she invited huskily.

'Do you promise to love and honour me, Catia *mia*?'

'Yes, oh, yes.' She was trembling, hungry for him as she'd never been hungry for any man before. Certain at last that he loved her.

His mouth descended to her throat, grazing the strong pulse that thundered the message of her arousal. 'Tell me, Catia, let me hear you say it—*con mio corpo ti adorero . . .*'

The words from the wedding service—with my body I will worship you!

Joyously she repeated them to please him, adding for full measure, 'Till death us do part.'

'*Bene*! Then you shall wear these again.'

He drew her reclining body into an upright position before releasing her to delve into the pocket of his jeans and produce the rings she had last seen on his pillow at the *palazzo*. 'Give me your hand, *carissima*.'

Carefully he replaced them on her finger. He was breathing heavily, a slight flush apparent on his high cheekbones. 'Now that you are once more happy to be my wife I think we should celebrate our reunion, *si*?' He laughed huskily. 'But not here. This place is more suitable for a peasant than a *marchesa* is it not?'

'Does it make any difference when you're in love?' she teased. 'But there's not a lock on the door and I fancy we've strained Richard's hospitality too long already. Do you think you can cope with the long walk back to Nonno's?'

'No.' Nicolò smiled wryly. 'But fortunately I won't have to. Once Antonio had told me what you had overheard and what you had assumed from it and convinced me that you still loved me, I drove down by hired car. If necessary I intended to kidnap you myself and hold you a prisoner in your grandfather's house until you surrendered yourself to me—body, heart and soul.'

'Should we say goodbye to Richard, do you think?' she ventured as he led her out into the yard.

'I think we should spare him that embarrassment,' he returned drily. 'It's going to be bad enough facing your grandfather and aunt as it is, with our intentions written so plainly on our faces!'

But the house was silent as they entered, and they walked quietly up the stairs to the bedroom Catia had used since Antonio Lorenzo had first brought her to what he saw as a safe haven. Confident that Paolo's son would be able to tame his wayward granddaughter, Antonio had persuaded Becky to serve coffee and pastries in the back garden, and had no intention of either of them re-entering the house until they were summoned to do so by his grandson-in-law.

There was no need for preliminaries. Already their bodies were tuned for love, joining together, renewing their intimate knowledge of each other as soon as the barrier of their clothes had been discarded by eager fingers. Nicolò took Catia with all the power and finesse of which his fine male body was capable, and she welcomed him as her lover warmly and generously, giving as well as taking until they hit the rising spiral of fulfilment together.

Bathed in the warm afterglow of satiation, Catia stretched languidly, trailing limp fingers across her husband's broad chest. In just over a week's time she would be standing beside him at the altar of Santa Maria dei Miracoli. How marvellous if Giuseppe and Gina Cabrini could be there—together!

Beside her Nicolò stirred lazily 'Cesare Brunelli,' he said.

'What?' she sat up abruptly.

Nicolò grinned. 'I was thinking of the wedding invitations. We mustn't forget Brunelli. He can give us a full-page spread—photographs of the wedding and the reception. He owes us that at least—what do you think?'

Catia laughed. 'I think you're the wickedest lover I've ever had!'

'And you're the most beautiful mistress who has ever graced my bed,' he retaliated in kind, lifting a strand of her fine hair to kiss it. 'My golden mistress—and my golden wife...hard fought-for, hard won...and mine forever!'